Take Your Shot

Your Blue-Collar Romance

RIA ZEN

Character Art: JE. Corbett Illustration
Book Design: Ria Zen

Second Edition
eBook ISBN 978-1-7770780-03
Paperback ISBN 978-1-7770780-1-0

Dedication

To the one plastered with labels that just won't stick,
you know who you are. Stand your ground.
<3

Chapter One

Benji

"You know what this calls for?" My devious grin stretches from ear to ear. Muscles strain and ache as I wait for my apprentice's answer. He's fresh blood, a high school graduate, who has the world at his fingertips, but totters around with his tail between his legs. Those toothpick legs straddle over where the customer's toilet once stood in the thirty thousand dollar plus powder room.

Justin stares at me wide eyed, horrified by my enthusiasm.

"You wanted to be a plumber, yeah?"

"A plumber, yeah. Not a freak!"

I waggle my eyebrows. "Come on…"

He shakes his head.

I clap my hands together and sway side to side to a make-believe tune.

"Stop. Please. Stop."

I don't, twirling towards the auger's switch. With a flick, my humming is drowned out by the sound of the tool as it works on unclogging the drain. I bob my head not missing a beat.

"Not the snake dance."

"Oh yes!"

Justin consciously exerts every possible attempt to ignore me, focusing on the task at hand.

"Ss-snake it!" Do I wiggle my butt? Of course! "In deeper, down the hole then give it a wiggle… then a jiggle."

"Heck, man. Do you hear yourself?"

"Up. Down. Wiggle then jiggle. Say it with me, wiggle then jiggle."

"No."

"A wise guy, eh?" Humour is how we handle the job. Gotta keep it light for the literal crap shows we deal with on a regular basis. It's gnarly work. No one wants to do it, but that's why they pay us triple the cost to get it done. Soon enough, he will see I'm doing him a solid and perhaps create a silly dance of his own. I glance at his dark washed jeans in disappointment. Mine are made with a durable canvas material, covered in all sorts of stained crap… literal, figurative too with the dried ABS glue, and large swatches of silicone on my thighs, making water resistant patches.

I don't get it. Is he trying to be a pretty boy? We switch spots, unintentionally leaving muddy prints on the marble floors. At least he's wearing rubber boots, although he should invest in a more durable pair, like my steel-toes. They're a requirement for a reason. I'd hate for him to have a slip-up when he's this early in the game.

"Lighten up. One day while you're clearing drains, it will become second nature to you."

He snorts. "Benji, I can't imagine why you're single."

"It's my good looks, I assure you," I say sarcastically. I'm going to embrace who I am. If the world can't handle the gritty truth that this is me, if I'm not good enough for them then too bad. Beggars can't be choosers. I have my friends, a lot of them, a lot of lady friends too. None of them have kissed me, but I'm not going to embarrass myself to try harder for something I'll fail to achieve.

Justin rolls his eyes. "Blonde or brunette?"

"I don't play this game, because I don't play girls." I'm not what they're looking for so I might as well skip the trauma altogether. My heart has been through enough for one lifetime. Everyone knows I'd choose friendship over something sexier. I'll suppress my drive to make a girl swoon, so hearts aren't broken, including mine. The snake catches onto the source of the clog.

"How did your date on Friday go?" I ask.

"The walk was alright. I thought it was going to be boring, but she held my hand the whole time and..."

See? I smirk in an 'I told you so' manner.

"First kiss of many," he says.

Ending the dance, I pat his shoulder congratulating him. The snake pulls out what was once a tampon. Justin pretends to hurl into his elbow.

Justin gags at the stench. I lift my bucket for him, but thankfully it's a false alarm.

Unlike Tuesday.

I cross my arms. "Get used to it. Mice are the number one cause of toilet clogs." Our eyes shift to the gold trash can underneath the toilet paper hook. Sheesh, some people have money to burn... or waste.

"*Blonde* or brunette?"

"Bald, if it means I get a personality, and no. I'm not dating your sister." Nor am I interested in dating anyone! Leave me be!

"But she's twenty-two and you're like twenty... seven?"

Thirty next month. Once he catches a whiff of never happening, he turns to me.

"What now?"

"What do you mean, '*what now?*' Reinstall the bloody toilet. You think Ms. Ellis wants to piss on the floor after we charge her a whopping hundred bucks an hour?"

He does a fine job. I give him more flack than he needs, but there's nothing worse than bad plumbing. I have him wet a rag and hand mop the mud (one can never be too sure what it is in this field) off the heated tile floor. I sling my toolbag over my shoulder. He carries the rest. He's a young, tall, strapping man. Me, well... to him, I'm old.

Like my last apprentice, he will probably have a new girl under his arm each month, maybe each week. I'd rather skip the heartache. Finding dates, grooming up, charming the other… It's work, worth it for some, but not all romantics find their other half. I'll be fine.

Approaching Ms. Ellis in her living room drinking tea and reading a novel peacefully, I wait for her to place her book down, so I can update her on the situation. She folds her reading glasses and rests them precariously on the creased paperback cover.

"You unclog toilet, yes?"

"I speak English." Fluently. I grin wide to mask my frustration. My grandparents were the immigrants, not me. The rest of us have our citizenship. I grew up in this town. Why are people like this, still? "Yes I did. There was a tampon."

Her face becomes beet red. "I don't know how it... that was it? It wasn't..."

I shrug.

"Thank... you."

Geez woman, I speak English! "The bill will arrive in the mail, unless you stop by the shop and pay this week. Later." *See you in a month, two tops?*

My phone rings as Justin follows me into the work van. It's Juan, my younger brother. His contact picture is of me hoisting him via wedgie back when he was in grade school. I smirk. As an older brother, it's my civil duty to humble him. His boss stole him for a carpentry apprenticeship before he could join me. Apparently Juan didn't care for the dynamic duo aspect, as the sub-trades aren't versatile enough... according to him.

"Our plumber had an emergency call."

No. Your idiot head plumber is hungover, ditching this bid to take on cash jobs for quick money to pay for his habit. I warned Juan's boss about him, but he played it off as if I was scrounging for business. My schedule is full. That's what happens when a person does their job, and they do it well. If anything, we need plumbers more than ever.

"Are you available?"

"Can be. What am I looking at?" I say, checking the time.

"New construction."

"Cool. I'll bring Justin with me." If my apprentice can't handle it, he isn't up for the blue-collar life. He still has to learn he can't dance out of some situations, even if he wishes he could.

"Did you get the board stretcher?" I ask Justin, fishing for my car keys. His eyes go wide, then he frantically hurries back into the customer's house. I overhear him hum the tune to the snake song on his way out.

Eventually everyone falls in love with the snake dance. I only hope he learns the easy way. Trades can be tough on a man, but it can also shape them.

Juan and I end the call.

Justin returns empty handed, but his little search gave me enough time to update the office.

We drive to the address Juan sends me, turning onto the dirt driveway and narrowly squeeze in between the pickups under the shaded patch of the trees. Here I was hoping to finish the day early, but instead we're installing a shower head.

Assessing the task, I turn to my apprentice, "I'm sure this will be quick." I walk over to Juan and borrow his skill saw. "I'll make the backing; you set up the other pieces."

I place the board on the sawhorses outside, mark my measurements with my pencil then tuck it by my ear. It bumps the silver forward helix, my favourite earring. Like my buddy's view on tattoos, I really can't get enough metal. I love it, been tinkering with the idea of having my tragus done—both sides. I've thought about tattoos, but I can't decide on what in particular. But piercings? Stab away.

The sun's ridiculously bright today, but it does little to dry the thick trenches of mud around the property. Squatting low to the mud, I fish out the extension cord too close to a puddle.

Idiots.

Plugging the saw in, I carry it to the boards resting on the sawhorses, then I whip the cord away from my marked cut. Gliding the skill saw along the two-by-four, Juan's journeyman with his fat behind passes by and bumps my board. My handling slips and the saw grazes the base of my thumb.

"Agh—" I spell out the English alphabet in a vivid rainbow of profanities, dropping the skill saw onto the ground. My excessive words are like a gunshot in the forest, disturbing the peaceful flock of birds.

"Whoa man, you okay?"

I squint at the fumbling idiot, clutching my bleeding hand. Through gritted teeth I cuss him out too. "—you! Watch where you're going, you stupid..."

More guys run outside to follow the commotion, not that my use of vocabulary is ever a shock to the Jackson & Reiss carpentry crew. Juan pushes through the guys, looks down at me. Because that's what every older brother wants... their younger yet taller brother worrying over them. But I can't hide the fact I'm dripping blood on my boots, the lumber, the ground... it's everywhere.

"Just get me Krazy glue and duct tape." And some drugs. I can't cry like a baby girl in front of Juan. He will never drop it. I'm sure I have some ibuprofen in the van. At my age and this many years in service, I need them to survive. My knees have as much structural integrity as a plastic bag of loose LEGO.

"Benji, no. We're taking you to the hospital."

I shake my head. "Nah, nah. It's fine. Just some blood. I'll find a rag and..." Who doesn't get blood on their tools from time to time?

"No. You'll infect it."

"Where's the first aid guy?"

"I am the first aid guy and I say I'm driving you to the ER to confirm it really is nothing."

We head to my work van. Juan jumps into the back, hunting through the mess for an unused rag. I lean in. "Must've used the last one at the Ellis'."

"That guy's ex-wife is so weird."

"You'd think after snaking their drains this often, she'd stop thinking we were immigrants."

"She only thinks you're an immigrant." Juan points to my chest. "Shirt. Mine's sweaty."

"But we're brothers." I unbutton my shirt the best I can with my one decent hand. He assists sliding it off my arms and binds it around my hand and wrist. "Her daughter was in your class." She fell for his good looks and they made out every lunch hour for a week.

"Maybe she thinks you're adopted." Juan slams the back doors and hops in the driver's seat. I hand him my keys with my non-bloody hand, but I deny his theory. We have the same thick dark hair, brown skin, and eyes. Only he has the mysterious squint that has all the ladies convinced he's a male model. The idiot is blind to the charm he has over them.

Unlike me. No model looks.

Due to years of stress and a certain traumatizing event, I've had to spend the last year on a strict diet and exercise regime to burn off all that comfort eating. I've worked my butt off, again literally and figuratively. Forty-three pounds lost in the last eight months and I still don't have a six-pack like Juan's. My stomach is flat enough. On a good day, with the right pose it's maybe a soft T. Not dad-bod! I repeat, I do not have a dad-bod! Some men aren't born demigods, some of us have to work at it.

At the hospital, Juan and I sit in the waiting room for nearly an hour. We watch stunt fail videos off his phone using the hospital's slow WiFi. It's painful. By the third video, we switch to data.

"Benjamin Gakhar?" The five foot nothing greying nurse searches the faces in the room. I stand. He motions me to enter. Turning to my brother, I purse my lips to prevent a chuckle. He looks exactly like the dwarf warrior from Lord of the Rings.

I nod to my brother. "Thanks. You can take the work van if I'm more than ten minutes." I won't be. Gimli's double will wash me up, give me a Tylenol and send me out the door.

The nurse directs me to a side room. I take a seat on the bed, leaning forward to not stain the periwinkle sheet. "Another nurse will be with you in just a minute, Benjamin."

"Benji."

The nurse slants his eyes and tugs the curtain shut.

Chapter Two

Hannah

I disassemble my paper cup and drop each component into their designated recycling bins: the cup and sleeve in the cardboard slot, then the lid with the plastic. Next I head to the bathroom, force myself to go then wash my hands. Coincidentally, anytime during my shift I may have had the chance, another patient usually waltzes in requiring immediate attention.

I'm working overtime today… again. This hospital has been short staffed for months. At least I will have Monday off. The first one in what feels like a very long time. I told my scheduler it is non-negotiable and I have big plans.

Gourmet brunch. Bacon, eggs, fruit salad, hash browns, pancakes, yogurt... I want it all. I've been fantasizing about it all day.

I fix my ponytail and adjust the bobby pins to tuck those pesky stray strands of my blonde hair back into place. In the mirror, I notice it's too far left and there's a pinch of loose strands free at my neck. Yanking the elastic out, I retie it until my hair is held high and centered like it should be. My phone beeps. My break is over.

I wash my hands again, then upon entering the ER nurse's station, I wave my hand under the automatic sanitizer dispenser and massage the foam thoroughly in and around my hands and wrist until dry.

"Glove up," Steve says. "Behind curtain number one we've got a herpes patient and behind curtain number two an injured tradesman needing an assessment for compo."

I resist the urge to scratch my eyes. The coffee was no help whatsoever. "Curtain, herpes, assessment... got it." I repeat back to him, slapping on the blue nitrile gloves. If it was sanitary, I'd slap my cheek to wake up. That break was virtually useless. If I don't recharge soon, I'm going to become one of those patients behind the curtain.

"And the doctor?" I ask, technically we're supposed to have one on the floor at all times, but just like nurses, we're short on white coats too.

"Finishing up a delivery."

"Got it."

Steve hands me the clipboard, which I pinch to my side with my elbow.

Stepping through the closest curtain, I stare down at the clipboard. "Benjamin Gakhar, sorry for the wait. Our doctor will be here momentarily, but I'm going to go ahead and ask you the same questions until then." The rings screech along the track as I drag the curtain for further privacy. "Tired? Sore?" I ask.

"Tell me about it… and it's Benji."

"No. Actually I need you to tell me about it. How long has this been bothering you?" I click the pen.

"Uh… maybe an hour."

I glance up from the papers. "An hour?" Usually something like this doesn't reveal itself for a couple days. He's sitting on the edge of the cot. My eyes skim his jet black hair. The sides are buzzed, yet there's fullness up top as if he combs it up with his fingers constantly. I've seen a lot of patients, but never have I seen such thick hair. It's incredible. Rather than standing straight, the strands flop over in a voracious swirl. Piercings cover his ears with moderately sized spacers in his lobes. His five o'clock shadow seems scratchy, yet I slow down my inspection at his massive biceps beneath those weighty shoulders, like shoulder pads under a jersey. His muscles are thick and solid with a generous coating of that illustrious man-fuzz. With looks like those, his diagnosis makes sense.

Stop that thought right there, Hannah. The guy's a player and he has herpes.

But he's shirtless.

Mmm…

Clipboard, yes. I hold it up, using it as a wall between us. "Date of birth?"

"Next month," he quips, flashing me a toothy side-grin.

"Numbers, Benji." Year. Month. Day. I fight the urge to snap my fingers impatiently, so I creep up a weak but forced smile. It's been a rough day and I've already passed my breaking point four hours ago. "Could you be more specific?" I say in my nice voice. Though I love my job, I don't love the frequent shifts that run into overtime. It isn't his fault my break didn't release the tension from the last patient's heart failure.

Or the patient before's poopslosion.

He gives me the exact date.

Huh, we're close in age. Neat.

"Feverish?" I ask.

"A bit."

Me too. I press my lips into a firm line. His eyes go wide with concern.

"Oh, is that bad? Is it infected?"

"Possibly. Have you been having regular bowel movements?"

"I guess?" He raises one of his thick dark eyebrows. "Is that related to my current condition? I've been eating healthier, I drink lots of water..."

I stifle a snort. Drinking water will not cure him from the consequences of his promiscuous activities. "Any discomfort with urination? Any pain, stinging, discolouration?"

"Pain yeah, but not—"

"How would you rate the pain, from one being a hard poke to a ten being the worst pain fathomable?" I ask. Assessing me, he quips up a playful smirk. Ugh! I could care less how macho he thinks he is, I need to figure out the intensity of his condition. "Honestly."

"Eight."

"Okay, is it burning or..."

"Nah, my brother rubbed the area clean after it happened."

I tilt my head, locking onto his eyes baffled by his comment. His brother?

He gulps. "It's not infected, is it?"

"We will find out after we examine the area. Did you notice any blisters or lesions?"

"No?"

"Are there any issues with the plumbing besides..." Usually I hate this part of my job. Usually. What matters is the patient receives the help they need, even if I want to go home and have a good cry.

"No issues. I have years of experience. I'm really good at what I do, I swear. These kinds of things don't happen to me. I'm careful… it was the other person who wasn't."

Cancel that. He's handsome, but experience is no charm. Player. He's a player. *Remember Hannah, he's a player*. I have to stop ogling the hair, his twinkling eyes, that charismatic smirk...

"I'm sure you do. When was the last time you..." my question falls short. Why are my cheeks flushed? It must be the building. Hospitals are often set to a higher temperature. I'll have to drink more water when I have the chance. Just ask the handsome stranger about his sexual activity. *Toughen up, girl. You do this all the time.* I should avoid slang to ease the awkward tension. *Get straight to the point. Stop wondering if he is interested in you. Ask him directly about his sexual activities.*

"Uh... what? The guy bumped me hard, but it was an accident."

I stifle my disappointing groan. Oh. That's unfortunate. From his confidence, he must be a frequent flyer too. Such a shame, he's such a... I was hoping he... not hoping, but he seemed... huh. Why am I disappointed? *Player! Remember?* It should not matter.

"When?" I ask. I don't care for stories. The less I know on the subject at hand, the better. If this patient could please answer the question as it's my primary concern for the well-being of his... him, what's best for him. Yes, clipboard. I hold it to my face, avoiding his grin. As if I'm the one who needs to be comforted or wooed. The only thing I need is food and sleep.

"Less than an hour ago." During the day? I peek another glance at him, still smirking at me all smug. *Stop being the epitome of stereotypical manliness; I have a job to do! Ugh!*

"Any protection?"

"Steel toe boots and safety glasses, I guess."

I raise my eyebrows, refusing to glance up from the clipboard. Surprisingly not the strangest kink I've heard of in these four walls. "I thought I had a firm grip, but he pushed the wood hard enough to knock my balance. Then *zing*, this happened."

"Your mouth too?" I ask before his details become unnecessarily graphic.

He shakes his head.

"Anal?" The colour drains from his face as if he's about to lose his dinner.

"Do you use condoms?"

"No?" His jaw drops and his head tilts to the side like the cogs are turning in his mind. Again that smug grin of his returns. "Are you supposed to?"

I stare at my feet and take a deep breath. "Yes." Exhale. *Don't play dumb, Benjamin Gakhar.* I don't flirt with boys at work and I'm not giving him an in depth explanation on how to use them or answer his asinine questions for his perverted form of entertainment. Personally, I prefer to find men outside the ER. No coworkers, no patients, and absolutely no handymen. "I'll grab the doctor in a moment here, but I'll need you to drop your pants. Here is your gown and I'll give you some privacy—"

"Drop my what?"

"Your pants. We need to confirm the infection before they can administer the anti-virals."

"Sorry, what?" his says louder.

"Your pants. Benji, don't shoot the messenger okay? If it looks like a duck, sounds like a duck—"

"Then it's a—"

"You've got herpes," I say, cringing at myself for how upfront I was. I'm sorry! I should have said it with far more bedside manner or left it for the doctor, but the words spewed out and often the 'active' guys in this situation are exasperating. Trust the professional. He fooled around, now he's caught red… groined.

"What the…"

I point to the poster behind me.

"Language-free zone," I inform him, lowering my clipboard and my gaze. "Your boyfriend might not be too thrilled with the news." I doubt my forced smile or genteel tone has saved this blunder. I might as well say goodbye to my career too. When word gets out, I'll be jobless. My focus locks on to the grey shirt wrapped around his left hand. "What happened to your hand?"

"I just told you. Though, if it's *absolutely necessary* to strip down, I may need your assistance," he says, waving his covered hand. "Literally."

My mouth gapes. I return to the clipboard, actually reading it instead of pretending to. I'll bet I'm blushing cardinal red. I don't have to see it to know. I'm burning up. He unwinds the shirt. The inside is soaked with blood. I swear his smirk twitched with amusement.

"As a professional, of course... since I am incapacitated." Oh congratulations, he used a big word in the proper context. Judging by his dirty canvas pants and mud soaked boots, I bet it was a fluke. Could he stop staring at me like that? This isn't a joke, but being professional means, I can't smack him with my clipboard, so I plaster on another fake smile right over the previous one.

"My bad. Let's clean that and stitch you up."

"Are you going to ask your *girlfriend* for help?"

"Ha. Ha. Very funny."

"Do you still want me to drop my pants?"

Ahem, well...

He waggles his eyebrows.

"No." Exhale. "Let's start over. How did you cut yourself?" I begin to wash his wound. Let's start over and hope he extends grace in my direction, shall we?

"Skill saw."

"Ouch."

He shrugs, like it's no biggie, like I needed more evidence of Benji's masculinity. His toned chest lined with a soft pelt of hair wasn't enough?

"When was the last time you had your tetanus shot?"

"Uh, it's been a while."

"Be more specific."

"Probably elementary school." Benji flinches when I treat the wound site. "I don't keep track of those things."

"I'll check with your file. Any allergies I should know about?"

"Bees and wasps."

"The freezing should be fine then. What exactly do you do for a living, Benji?" Maybe I could lighten up the mood a smidge to distract my patient from realizing the ramifications of his bleeding.

"Plumber."

Not a gay prostitute, good. That will decrease his chances of herpes significantly. With a second glance, I can't picture him to be one to go to town. He has great hair, but other than that, he doesn't match the stereotypes.

But a plumber? How disappointing is that? Why was I hoping he'd have at minimum half a brain? That's my job though, isn't it? Fixing Neanderthals who think that if they can hold a wrench, they should be trusted with something sharp. How dangerous could plumbing be? Aren't they paid to plunge toilets?

It explains why I was feeling on edge around him. This patient is just like my ex-boyfriend and why I hate everything about men like him. Guys like them, they're always messing around, avoiding safety procedures, and showing up here on a weekly basis. And can't they wash their hands or use a rag? Why are they blackened with grease? Being covered in dirt is supposed to be repulsive. It's bad hygiene and probably the reason guys like this Benji are stuck plunging toilets, when they could actually try to be decent human beings. He could be more than a sleazy pickup artist who thinks talking about his power tools will cause me to swoon. *Get over yourself, Benji.* If he used his brain, maybe he wouldn't have to rely on his toolbelt to have a fulfilling relationship with a member of the opposite sex.

"You?" He pauses to read my name tag. "Hannah, do you get paid to tell people they have herpes then jab them with needles?"

After freezing his arm, I thread the surgical needle. "Sometimes."

"You ask a lot of men to drop their pants?"

"We don't tolerate sexual harassment." *Don't prod him.* He is a horny tradesman who is going to flirt incandescently. I'm a nurse, not a male fantasy. Two can play at this game. Who's the one fixing his hand? I wish I could talk back with, "You're a mouthy plumber dumb enough to cut himself with a skill saw." Only I do say it and it's too late to take it back.

No!

His smile withers and his deep voice turns as cool as steel, "I'm not dumb. It was an accident."

It always is. I roll my eyes. He squints at me.

"I liked you better when I had herpes. Do you have a problem with plumbers?"

I avoid his piercing glare. "Nope." But I've yanked enough nails out of tradesmen and stitched enough labourers to defend my argument. My ex-boyfriend is a mechanic and ridiculously accident prone. Unfortunately, I saw him first thing this morning, second time this month, because he waited all weekend to claim his twisted elbow for worker's compensation. His surprise visits at the hospital have never been romantic. Each scar was another funny story to him.

This girl wasn't laughing. The joke is over. I dumped him.

And none of his one-liner innuendos would charm me this time. I'd like a man with a brain and the ability to use it.

Three stitches later, I snip the excess thread. "Don't skill saws have a safety feature so this doesn't happen?"

"That's not how the safety guard works on a tool. I still have my hand, don't I?"

"Fair enough. You'll need to see your doctor in two to three weeks to remove the stitches. Keep the area clean, covered, and try not to put any strain on it."

The ER physician enters the room, runs through the same questions excluding the mishap, repeating my advice. I walk past the curtain, returning to the nurse's station as they crack a couple light-hearted jokes.

"Juan's your brother? Interesting name. I take it Gakhar isn't Spanish?" the doctor says.

"No. My mom was obsessed with Spanish soap operas when she was expecting him. Dad tried to talk her into a more traditional name, but like my sister and I, Dad succumbed to the requests of his lover of twenty-nine years now. How long have you been married, Doc? Fourteen, fifteen years?"

"Eighteen, actually."

Benji slides the curtain open. "Eighteen? Wow! Good for you." He glances down to his bandaged hand, admiring it. "She did a good job, huh. Precise. Even spacing... neat and tidy."

My eyebrows perk. How can he tell? His thumb is covered in gauze and this isn't his profession. Is he teasing me? Really? How dare he question my abilities! Those stitches are perfect. I accept nothing less.

Out of sight, I droop down, nearly touching my toes and let out a long exhale. That couldn't have been any more embarrassing. Fingers crossed, he will forget all about me and move along with his day. I never mess up. Never. I hope I will never have to see that patient ever again.

Chapter Three

Benji

I peer around the door for one final glance at Hannah. Why do the hot ones have to be evil? And since when do scrubs actually look flattering? They used to be boxy and came in only three colours. But her slim fitting turquoise scrubs are... not half bad. Her high ponytail bounced with her sashay, giving off that preppy cheerleader vibe too.

I bite my lip to thwart a wolf whistle.

Herpes!

Out of all the labels and assumptions slapped on me, this one is new. Wait until the guys at the shop hear about this. Wait until her basement floods, who will be laughing then?

She thinks she has me all figured out now, does she? Because what? Because I'm a plumber, like that's all I am? Her snide eye roll. Her demeaning scowl. What did I do wrong? How am I the one to blame? The Krazy glue and pain meds would have done the trick. I don't need her nasty judgements. Her icy blue eyes dissected every inch of me with a grimace so wound up her gnawed lip nearly bled.

Rude.

I'm not the idiot here. I'm not the one who misdiagnosed a bleeding man to have an STI. Where did that come from? What gave her that impression? How do I appear as an active contributor of the... I am most definitely straight!

One look at her proved it. Where did she go... not like it matters. My 'relationship type' is NA, not applicable. I am going to remain a bachelor. This does not mean I don't think she is attractive.

Physically, everything is beyond exceptional, but I'm not shallow. If I were to date it would be with a woman I could have meaningful conversations with, someone worth holding an umbrella for in the rain. If I mate, I mate for life. This nurse is not that woman. The rain can douse her for all I care. Especially if she falls for the plumbers are dumb pigeonhole. She doesn't know me!

Insufferable.

Who knew the devil had blue eyes and perky breasts.

Juan drives me to my place so I can have a quick shower before we head to Mom and Dad's. My house is an average three bedroom one bath beginner home close to downtown. Since moving in, I've made the immediate repairs, but that's it. Home is supposed to be a break from work. Who cares if the bathroom is lime green, and the kitchen is sky blue with dark oak cabinets and brass hardware.

I have made a few changes around the place. Juan and I reshingled the roof last summer out of necessity and I built the deck of all decks this last month in time for barbeque season. It's like a birthday gift to myself. That is the extent of my major renovations. Paint, flooring, preferences, they can all wait until I care.

Not today. Probably not tomorrow. The important thing is that it functions.

I slip into shorts and a comfortable yellow t-shirt that reads, 'Never argue with a plumber; they know their…' then it has my favourite word on the planet. Can't miss it. Seems fitting. Though I wish I was wearing it in front of her Royal Highness, Miss Hannah of Know-It-All Land. Too bad I'm the totalitarian dictator of Isle Don't Give a Crap. Albeit the asterisk seems redundant.

Juan finishes his text then slips his phone back in his pocket, as I buckle up. Apparently getting stitches is the same as having cancer to Mom, so I'm invited over for dinner.

"Are you sure you want to wear that?" he asks me.

"Do I care?"

Juan wraps his arm behind my headrest and reverses out my driveway.

"*Sat sri akal*," I greet my parents in Punjabi, I only know a few words but it's the little things to keep our grandmother from disowning us boys. Not that she lives with my parents anymore, but some things just stick. Grandma rarely spoke English, so us kids were accustomed to listening to her punjabi growing up. She moved out when Juan was little, so the extent of his vocab is *yes, no, thank you*, and *playground*. It's not my culture, but they insist it is.

Our sister, the favourite, had to of course move to India to tutor English at some ritzy university, but the dedicated workaholic that she is, decided to spend her summer vacation time in the remote villages teaching ESL as a volunteer. She has some multi-step plan on increasing her chances for a promotion, and ideally gaining recognition. The university gig already pays well and she plans on visiting during the Christmas holiday season.

Juan says she's seeing someone but hasn't told Mom yet. Apparently he's your typical bore, another campus professor with traditional values. I think she should dump him to prioritize her career. Why settle for domestics and baby-making after all the effort she has exerted for her peers' respect?

She won't listen.

We don't talk much.

Always flirting with the white-collars… that's my sister.

I refuse help from Juan with my coat. The jacket has a zipper, it's not rocket science. We kick off our boots and greet Dad in the living room. He's fixated on the baseball game, since hockey is off-season.

"Homerun!" he whoops, his fist swirling enthusiastically in the air.

Juan crashes on the couch next to his easy chair. Two years into his apprenticeship working hard, yet I'm not convinced he's moving out anytime soon.

"I could use a hand if..." Dad says, lifting his arm out. I steer his wheelchair closer, prepping to shift him from chair to chair.

"It's not that bad," I mumble, but that's probably because the drugs are in effect. "My hand is fine. It's just a few stitches."

"What happened to your hand?" Mom hollers. Juan told her, but she wants to hear it from me, like it's an elaborate story for when she meets with her friends later in the week.

"I was bumped using the saw. It's just a nick. I'm fine." She's not thrilled that both her boys ditched the white-collar dream for the trades.

Mom rants in Punjabi while stirring whatever meal she is making. It simmers on the stove and the aroma is heavenly. Something about how I should be safer. I shouldn't work with dangerous tools. What did she do wrong? She's never going to have grandchildren. What noble woman would be attracted to a man who could but chooses not to work up the ladder? Why couldn't I be a better example to Juan?

"*Mainu maaf karo.*" I'm sorry I didn't want to be an engineer, doctor, lawyer… whatever. Sorry I'm a cussing plumber, but it pays the bills. And as much as Mom disagrees with the big man, Dad says handiwork is men's work.

Turning to Dad, I assist him into his wheelchair with my good arm for support. "What's for dinner?"

"Ginger carrot soup."

"Who's sick?"

"You, apparently." Dad pokes at the asterisk on my yellow shirt, not impressed with the use of profanity. "Seem fine to me. Let's eat."

I bite my tongue. Age holds no boundaries from my mom giving me a lashing for bad mouthing anything. Juan relaxes into the pillow cushions with his knees up, resting the phone on his lap, while he texts away.

"I'm going to watch the game," he says.

Dad scowls at Juan with a '*get your butt to the dinner table*' glare. Juan groans, slides his phone into his pocket, the immaturely rolls off the couch. He sluggishly finds his seat at the dinner table.

"You texting that Jenny chick?" I prod him with the bowl of crackers. "You like her?"

He shrugs disinterested. "She's hot, I guess. What about you?"

I roll my eyes. *Don't get me started.* Girls aren't attracted to men like me. They want Juans. Good-looking, bend-over backwards for the freshest meat imbeciles. They want young, stupid, and rich. Or they want white men with waxed chests, clean shaves, and noose ties in black suits. Too handsome, too rich.

Romance is dead.

Long gone are the days of sneaking up to a fair maiden's bedroom window with a rose, promising a late night of fun and adventure. Today that's called trespassing, stalking, harassment... possibly abduction, and coercion. What about sending love letters even if we live nearby, because who doesn't love receiving physical mail? Or agreeing to watch a poorly produced romance film with a half-baked plot, so I could hold her in my arms uninterrupted for a couple hours?

Why should I go through all that effort, if I'm going to screw that up too? Seems I can't even hold a saw.

Dad gestures for Mom and whispers in her ear. He pushes on the wheelchair's armrests and lifts his body to reach her cheek for a soft peck.

Juan returns to his phone screen. The text-flirting... case and point. Jenny and Juan are going nowhere any time soon. Love is risky, but touch is sexy. Appearances can be deceiving. One day he will figure it out.

Words are sound, without action they hold no meaning. Swoon. Seduce. Savour. It is the romance trifecta. It should be intimate and relational, not crude. The experience of all three should be first-hand and in the flesh. Girls don't want short brown hairy men with dad-bod. They want men with a British accent and proper speech, not a dirty mouth.

"Girls like a clean man, not a man covered in crap. Case and point." I point to myself. "Still single." Despite the shower, I probably smell—not that I can smell anymore. I've been exposed to enough fumes I bet my nostrils have been permanently damaged.

Mom glares at me.

"*Mainu maaf karo.*" I'm sorry... but it's true. Nookie not dookie. Nobody's going to settle for a man who's full of crap. I know who I am. I'm content, but it's not what women want in a husband, so let's avoid the heartbreak and skip the risk. It's not that I won't try. It's because I know I will fail. They don't need that type of negativity in their life. I can handle my problems. It's my mess. The shovel is in my hand.

"Oh Benjamin, you shouldn't be so down on yourself." Mom stirs the spoon in her bowl and blows on it.

I grunt. Just because Mom thinks I have potential, it doesn't mean others will view me the same.

"Some girls like a dirty man." Okay, now she is pushing it. She hates my career path. Did I mention she hates my job? Oh did I forget to say Mom hates that I'm a plumber? If I didn't, Mom hates what I do for a living. She hates it. Hate. Not dislike... hate. The word is hate. Like how she hates my shirt, but more. My mom hates my job.

Every time I visit, "I saw you talking to that girl..." or "Any new friends? Oh. Does he have a sister?" or my personal favourite, "I was at a wedding. You will never believe who I bumped into... and she happens to be single."

"Mom!" Juan covers his ears. "Gross!"

I smirk. Yeah, no offense, but she is not the person I want dating tips from. I'm not dipping into that pool. Single for life. Thank you.

Dad chuckles. He extends his arm, resting his hand on hers. He was a truck driver until the accident. With a hooded gaze, Mom melts on the spot, and it mutes her on the subject. They share an R rated conversation with their eyes alone.

I clear my throat.

Juan, oblivious, texts Jenny under the table, his lip occasionally twitches upward.

Mom and Dad seduce each other with more blinks and winks.

We eat in silence, which is weird. Mealtime is usually louder, or has some noise of some sort. I prefer when people talk, argue even. I'm out.

The second my bowl is empty, I race out the door. "*Sat sri akal!*" I holler on my way out. Yep, I'm not welcome anymore. With my jacket hanging over my shoulder I double-check my house keys are in my pocket. A long walk should cool me off. Exercise is good, whenever I can squeeze it in. It has been a long week.

Flowers border the stone path leading to the broken sidewalk. Roses, peonies, marigolds, pansies. The path is vivid with colour, buzzing with activity. Why Mom bothers with curb appeal in this rundown area of town, I have no clue.

A bug buzzes around my hair. Ugh! It's the product, they like the fragrance, but it is super annoying, so I swat it away.

That's not a fly.

My left arm burns. I glance down to the bee stinger protruding out of my swelling skin. I'm red, puffing up.

"Mother—"

Juan pokes his head out the door as another bee stings me. My head throbs. The brick path spins around me. I taste the soup, the turkey sandwich I had for lunch, and vomit.

On the path, the plants, my feet… it's dripping between my toes, soaking through my sandals. *Not her flowers!* If I survive this, Mom is going to kill me.

I see two Juans, four, then hold my arm out to him. With my wavering vertigo and slippery foothold, I collapse onto the hedge.

Next thing I know, I'm in the emergency room—again, with Juan by my side and a killer headache.

Oh and the devil with her weapon of choice.

"Twice in one shift, huh Mario?"

Really, it couldn't have been any other nurse? Same turquoise scrubs, same perfectly centered ponytail, same icy cold stare.

Hannah turns to Juan. "And let me guess? Luigi?" She rolls her eyes, placing the used syringe in the biohazard trash can screwed against the wall. *Wow. What a beep!* At least let him embarrass himself before you slap on the names. Believe me, he won't disappoint.

"You play vid..." I pause to stabilize my focus onto one Hannah, not two. Imagine, two Hannahs? One is too many. I rub my eyes a couple times. "You play videogames, princess?" Makes sense, she seems like the internet troll type. Hating normal people for no apparent reason—very Hannah-the-nurse-from-hell. What's her gamer tag?

HotShot666? Please be a gamer. I want to boot her sprite off the screen like in Super Smash Bros.

"Nope. I'm too busy jabbing needles into a certain plumber." She grins. "I'll be back. Try not to cause any more trouble," then she winks. Am I hallucinating? Did she just wink at me? What twisted sense of humour does the devil have? Does she enjoy my presence or my misery?

"Wait!" I hold out my hand, motioning her to stop. Pivoting on her heel, her sneaker squeaks against the laminate floor. "Do you like my shirt?" I pinch the yellow fabric, ensuring the message is legible. She should take notes.

"Ironic."

"Ironic?" Man, she's a snarky one. Who poked the bear? Perhaps my smile irritates her. I'm enjoying pushing her buttons. Though I barely know her, her transparency is too amusing to pass up.

"If being a plumber means putting yourself in..." she clears her throat then uses air quotes, "*poopy* situations, I suppose the shirt could hold a kernel of truth to it. You're wearing yellow. You fell into flowers. I am not a brain surgeon, but that's... a story. So do you know your *poop*? No, not really."

"Well I guess I'll have to cross out plumbers for nurses, because clearly you know everything. Do you have a marker? I'll give you the honours." I puff out my chest to the best of my ability.

"A 'thank you' would have been appreciated." She pushes through the linen curtain.

Juan snickers, elbowing my side. "What did you do to piss her off?"

"Beats me." I close my eyes and fall back into the pillows.

"Why?" he says it like I'm oblivious to her features. "You get her number?"

"What? No." I don't do condescending airheads.

"But..." He motions his hands to mime her curves. Why does everything have to be about looks with him? Yeah she's pretty. So? This is why he has no friends. He has no patience. It's all surface level with him. Why would I be attracted to her? She didn't even like my shirt. It's a funny shirt. Who doesn't like funny shirts? Oh yeah, the stuck up HotShot666 beep, that's who.

"Dang it, Juan, I'm going to punch you the second I—"

An older brunette nurse pushes the curtain aside.

"Hey where's the other nurse?" I ask, poking my head around.

She shrugs, prepping the thermometer to test my temperature. "Her shift is over. Two bee stings. Severe allergy. How unfortunate," she states with a deadpan delivery.

Chapter Four

Hannah

Hot water burns my pale skin pink. I stand under the squealing faucet, inhaling the steam without a care in the world. I could stand here forever. Ah pure bliss. Monday is my day. No needles, no cleaning vomit, or slapping on gloves to yank out objects from where the sun doesn't shine.

This is the life.

Almost. I stare down at my feet at the shower base flooded with water. Oh lovely, a murky bubbly puddle.

Wash, rinse, repeat. The sudsy water pools over my toes, leaving a filmy residue on my skin. Ew!

Stepping out immediately, I reach for my phone and call my landlord… again. This has been going on for weeks, only now I'm home during decent hours and have time to deal with it.

"Did you not read my text?" he says.

"Uh no, why?"

"The plumber is on their way."

The doorbell rings, causing me to end the call abruptly and I'm only in a towel.

"One second," I holler, racing into my room to slip on whatever passes as an outfit, digging through what little I have left of clean laundry. I don't do unexpected visits; my job holds enough stress on its own. My sports bra curls over my torso, refusing to untangle while simultaneously suffocating me. I can tug all I want, but the silly thing isn't going anywhere. "Ugh! So not the time." I jump into skinny jeans that will not give. Hence why I never wear these clothes ever! Why have I kept them this long and why did I ever think now was the perfect time to bring them out?

Tripping over my pants, I mash my head against my mattress and flop onto the floor, like a baby giraffe when it's born. *Take a deep breath.* It feels like twenty minutes has passed when in reality, it has probably only been like two seconds. I slide on the glowing pink halter top I haven't worn since last summer, because it's the closest shirt on hand. Literally everything else is in the massive laundry pile desperately needing to be washed. Why did I buy this? It is obnoxious. I don't dare check out my reflection in the mirror. I don't have the time. Skipping the overall inspection, I rush to the entryway while tying my wet hair into a ponytail.

Every second counts.

Of course it isn't until I open the front door, that I realize I've put on my wedgie-inducing panties.

Great, just great.

They're riding. Ugh!

And look who's at my door, just like my landlord said.

Out of all the plumbers in this town, it had to be him. Is this a joke? He's supposed to be fat and greasy. He has the hairy thing down pat, except it suits him, amicably so. It looks so good on him.

Benji stares me down with such intensity I feel like I'm pinned to the wall. Though, not so much down, as across. He probably only has two or three inches of a height advantage, and I'm not tall.

"Mario."

"Peach," his voice softens with a smirk. This is going to be a slow and painful demise, isn't it? There is no denying he remembers who I am and the words I've said. I wish I hadn't, but we can't rewind the clock.

"The shower drain is clogged." My gaze travels, starting from his stained shirt with multiple rips and smears of hardened glue, up to his shaven face. A patch of hair lingers under his lip to compliment his sideburns. I preferred the scruff he had the other day. I wonder if he shaves twice a day.

Focus, Hannah.

His lips cheekily lift on one side. "Can't imagine why, Blondie."

I pout, self-consciously tugging at my ponytail. "You lack imagination, do you?" Blondie, princess, Peach. The fact he doesn't pick one and stick to it drives me bonkers.

"You wish." His gaze flits to the frilly lilac panties peeking out the bottom of my pant leg. I shake it out, kicking it into the air. With a simple swoop I bunch it into my fist. They were also a regrettable purchase. My roommate convinced me to purchase them. I've worn them once, and it was with these pants too. Never again. Go ahead, call me a prude. They weren't practical. But I'm keeping them, because they are cute, and they were really expensive.

"Hey, I told you to take it easy. What idiot gets himself in the ER twice in one day, no, one shift?"

Benji crosses his arms. His biceps bulge stretching his work shirt's sleeves. "I don't have to be here, you know. All it takes is a wire coat hanger and some creativity. If you have an imagination, you could do it yourself."

I pinch the bridge of my nose. Me? Unplug the drains on my day off? Okay fine, he has his field of expertise, I have mine. I can't believe out of all the tradesmen in this little town, he showed up.

"Stay." There it is. I admit defeat. Happy?

He winks as he walks past me, carrying his filthy toolbag to my closet sized bathroom. Clumps of dried mud break off his boots and fall onto the floor.

"It's not just the shower drain. The sink reeks, the toilet flushes slowly, I swear everything is wrong with this place. What's taken you so long?"

"I just got the call this morning. You're lucky I had a free slot between jobs. Most people have to wait a few days for something insignificant like this. That is if there's not an emergency somewhere else in town."

"Sure. Whatever. I wouldn't call myself lucky. I've been hounding my landlord all week. He said he called you, the first day."

"As much as I want to blame it on my infected boyfriend, the reality is, princess, you've got yourself a…" he spills out a profanity with ease.

"Language, Benji."

"A *bad* landlord," he corrects.

I ditch the thong into my bedroom hamper then lean against the door frame watching him take apart the drain. He shrugs unapologetically.

"This is my home and I won't accept your potty-mouth. It's unattractive and quite frankly gross. Foul language is never appropriate. All is proves is a lack of vocabu—"

"Who said anything about attraction?"

"Ew. I am not attracted to you."

"But I bet you like a man who talks dirty."

"Do not!" My cheeks flush.

He waggles his eyebrows. "Pass me the hand auger."

I squint, focused on his blackened hand. His callused palm is covered in healing cuts and around his knuckles are jagged blisters.

"The mini snake... forget it." He digs into his toolbag. "You should know, I charge double if you watch."

"Is that so?" "Why?" Is Benji going to sass me with rhetorical questions now? "You want a show or do you want this fixed?"

Both. I shake my head. I shift my balance to the other side of the doorframe and lean against the open door. After that comment, I'm definitely going to watch him snake the drain. At the moments I know for sure he is not looking, I pick at my wedgie.

He mischievously grins, peeling off his shirt.

"Wow. Real mature."

"I warned you, Peach. You're watching. You're getting a show." A few minutes later, he pulls out the main clump of hair. I wonder how often he has to clear the drains. Like is this all he does? Where did those muscles come from?

When he catches me watching, I look away, witnessing my face matching the colour of my outrageously obnoxious top.

"This is not professional," I sputter, flicking my hair to the side.

"Depends what you're paying me for." He winks.

If he keeps winking at me like that, I'm going to make him see a doctor. It must be a neurological twitch. Brain injury is no laughing matter, but there's no other explanation to his incessant flirting.

"This of course coming from the *person...*" He bites his tongue as if he's holding back a curse or two. "...who accused me of limited intellect in a not so professional manner. You could call us even."

"Are you going to put your shirt back on?"

He shakes his head, enjoying how flushed I am over this. Angry. Yes this makes me feel angry, not the other reason my face would burn up.

"Are you a natural redhead?"

"My roommate."

"Ah." He dumps the wad of hair into the trash can. "Is she single?"

I laugh. "Never happening."

"Why? You think I'm pretty?" He rests his head over his hands like they're a platter and flutters his long lashes. Can't he wash his hands first? "You want me all for yourself?"

I laugh harder. My stomach aches. He's nasty. I haven't laughed this much in ages, and he isn't even trying. Me… want him? A plumber?

"Especially since you've seen all of this…" he gestures to his chest. "Twice now. You like it." He waggles his eyebrows. I glance away.

"Do not. I might actually miss that yellow shirt."

"Aha! So you did think it was funny."

"No. No. Not funny."

"What's next?" he asks. I point to the toilet. "Ah yes, slow flush? Let me have a look." He removes the tank lid, placing it carefully on the laminate floor. Benji pushes the lever, focusing on the flow of fresh water through the fixture, then groans. "You flush a tampon?"

"Never."

Benji proceeds to remove the toilet and snake out a tampon. He plunks it in the trash can on top of the wad of hair.

"Maybe your landlord isn't the problem."

On cue, my roommate enters the apartment.

"Ew, what is that smell?" Her grocery bags plunk onto our two–person dining table in haste to find us.

"This is that idiot I was—"

Stepping through the doorway, her voluptuous hip knocks me over. I grip onto a towel rod for dear life.

"*Hello.*" She licks the top row of her pearly whites, extending her hand.

Benji refuses.

"This is the second toilet I've had to unclog today."

I scowl. So it's okay to almost touch me but not her? How considerate of him.

He lifts his hands up in defence.

My roommate leans into my ear, "Is he for real or is there a hidden camera I don't know about?"

I nearly gag. Me. That? No. No. Nope!

"What?" he says defensively, "I was on call this weekend. Stop staring at my hand. It's healing fine." I point to his stitches, reminding him with my glare he was supposed to take it easy. "It's no biggie. Hi, I'm Benji. I'm a gay man with herpes."

Oh my... for the love of... are you serious?! I turn around and hide my face, smack it against the wall a couple times too while I'm at it.

My roommate's mouth gapes, unsure if he's serious or not. His straight face delivery is convincing. Stoic suits him well, if he would hold it. It has been smiles and frowns, nothing in between for me.

"Anyways, I have to dash out. Ashley and I are going shopping. Nice to meet you, Benji... with herpes?" She nabs her purse and ducks out, leaving me to put her groceries away.

I tug on my cheeks. "Can't you let that go?"

"Nah."

"Please."

"Nah."

"Ugh! What do I have to do for you to shut up about it?"

That wicked grin of his returns.

What did I just ask? Oh no. What have I done? He grazes his teeth over this lower lip. I won't ignore how I look or how he does sans shirt.

I swallow. Any chance he could fix the air conditioner? It's getting kind of hot in here.

"Admit I'm smarter than you."

Ha! Over my dead body!

I cross my arms and step forward. We're chest to chest, a hair—his pelt between us. With a snarl, I tilt up to face him, square in the eye. "If you're so smart then why are you a plumber?"

"Free country. I do what I want." Benji slings the toolbag strap over his shoulder. Without the shirt, the smears of pipe grease on his hands and up his forearms give me tingles. They add definition, highlighting his muscle tone in ways I never knew I wanted. My body acts against the wishes of my brain, eyeing him up, soaking every pore.

"You're not one of those immigrant doctors who lost their certification, are you?"

"I was wondering when the racist comments would come out of your chubby lips, *eh?* And no. I'm one hundred percent Canadian, born and raised, Blondie. Not me, you. You're Blondie." He flicks a loose strand of my hair behind my ear with the audacity to wink afterwards as if I didn't clue in he was labelling me an airhead. My hair colour has nothing to do with my level of intellect.

Flustered, I storm out of the bathroom, so he can fix the toilet alone. The faster he can work, the sooner he can leave.

They're not chubby, are they? I play with my lips in front of my dresser mirror. I'd change my clothes too, but that would be too noticeable for him. I'm not trying to impress anyone; I merely happen to be cursed with a stupid wedgie! It doesn't mean I can't brush my hair or quickly smear on a light coat of concealer, maybe some mascara or a touch of lipstick. My face needs colour.

A folded list pokes from underneath my makeup kit. Nostalgia hits hard when I read it. I wrote this in my teen years. I laugh at each one, because it proves how far off Benji is from each trait. What? A girl should have standards, and me? I'm organized. I have my list.

MR. PERFECT

1. TALL

2. CLEAN SHAVEN

3. NO PIERCINGS OR TATTOOS

4. FIT

5. RICH! LIKE WEARS A SUIT TO WORK RICH

6. CLEAN VOCABULARY.

There are twenty items on the list. Some I'll excuse, like preferring tea over coffee, since I live off of coffee now. This criterion is important to me, hence why everything is in capital letters. When I go off script, I pay dearly. Like my ex. I pushed my priorities aside and that failed big time. Following the list will fulfill the desires of my lonely heart. Why should I wander from it? If I never take big risks, I'm never hurt.

Flush.

Benji tests the bathroom sink. "Is sunshine supposed to have a scent?" he asks, exiting the bathroom while sniffing his hands. It's a potent soap, yet he treats the fragrance as if it is faint.

Go back in there and wash your hands again, you filthy man! In my line of work, any person who sniffs their hand exiting the bathroom should return, or steer clear from me. I squint at him, shoving the list under a jewellery box before he can ask about that too.

"Do you have a problem with a man who is good with his hands?"

"No." I shift my gaze to the blank wall, avoiding the temptation to look at him. Does he have X-ray vision? How? Did he see my paper? How did he know I was thinking about him? "Why aren't you wearing your shirt? I could report you." He completed the task. Button the shirt. Leave.

"I dare you."

"I will. And aren't you supposed to wear tan overalls?"

He chuckles, staring down to his black heavy-duty canvas work pants with his light grey underwear elastic exposed above the waist. Even with a belt, the tools in his pocket weigh them down.

"Preference. Overalls um... tug." Benji clears his throat, regaining my focus back to his face. "Did you mention a leak?"

"Reek. I said the kitchen sink reeks."

He intentionally brushes past me in the narrow hall, then empties the dishes from the sink and dumps potent chemicals down both drains. His gaze drips down to my hips.

Go ahead, take a picture!

He picks a blonde hair off my pant leg.

Oh. Whatever. That's not attention to detail, that's an excuse to touch me.

"Hey! You're supposed to wear a shirt."

"Not until you apologize."

"That isn't how apologies work."

"And what would you know about work? You know, *man*-ual labour. I can't imagine you busting your lady balls to be with a guy who's too prissy for basic home maintenance. Seems like you'll be stuck with me whenever you need a fix."

That blasted wink! Stop it! Stop grinning at me.

I can't help but be peeved by the emphasis on his pathetic pun. Most would hiss at him for being sexist, but the suave he holds as he pinches the toolbag's strap, sliding his fingers up and down, while holding eye contact... This is intentional, isn't it? With the realization his heated gaze brings, my cheeks flush. He's poking fun at me like I'm his new toy. Sorry buster, but I will not play that game. I grimace back at him, reminding him whose territory he's on. "Since when did this become about my dating preference?"

"Since..." he swallows, then checks his phone for the time. Cusses... no surprise there. "I should get going."

"No. No. Tell me."

"It's not. But if what I do is too dirty for you, then enjoy your sterile white-collar life."

"What I handle is anything but sterile."

"Ooh kinky."

I pout. "You're disgusting."

"Only when I want to be." Benji locks eyes with me again as his tongue polishes his right eye tooth.

"What's wrong with a white-collared man?"

"You tell me, princess. You're the one staring at my chest. Do I make you... uncomfortable?"

"Yes. Immensely so," I snarl bitterly, clenching my fists at my sides. Benji rushes to button his shirt while carrying his tools to the door.

"If you find your drains need servicing, call me, yeah?"

"What?"

"Get your mind out of the gutter, Hannah. I meant if the toilet's acting up again. And I'll talk to your landlord about buying a new showerhead. Not that it's my place, but hey that ancient relic ain't worth the CLR."

"Benji, I don't have your—"

In a ninja-like movement, he flicks out a business card from who knows where, bringing my hand closer to his. He lays it flat on my palm, and pats it down.

I flinch.

"Your hands are disgusting." Didn't he just wash them? Why are they still dirty?

"You like it." He winks as he leaves.

I glare vehemently at the black fingerprints on my white door then down to my open hand.

Chapter Five

Benji

My pulse is out of control. I'm confused and aching by the time I return to the shop to stock up on supplies for my next big job. Doug, the HVAC installer is banging away at sheet metal when I enter through the back door. He pauses.

"What's up?"

I'd rather not say. I'm still trying to process what happened.

"If you get a call from a blonde woman saying something about me strip-teasing or that I was sexual harassing her, don't believe her. She's crazy."

Doug lifts his eyebrows then returns to his ductwork. He pauses again and I know I'm in trouble.

"I didn't know you could determine hair colour through a phone call," the shop boy mutters.

I wave him the bird. The guy talks too much. I hope the boss fires him soon. He's not privy to the gossip. *Sweep, kid. You heard nothing.*

Did Hannah really have to wear a shirt that ridiculously bright? That is what we like to call a work hazard. I'm trying to be professional. And that skimpy piece of string, what was that? Despite my occupation, I seek to maintain a moderately clean mind or at least I try to bury those impulses under the rug. It doesn't help when industry jargon has been more informative than my high school sex education.

I can't believe what I said to Hannah. Did someone slip the blue pill in my coffee? What is going on?

Why the heck did I take my shirt off? It wasn't the heat, though it was hot there. But heck, she makes this too easy. Every word that slipped from my mouth made her blush a brighter pink, matching the shade of her tank top.

I've been in rough apartments, but never have I seen one of Walker's tenants keep their place that pristine. Of course a nurse would have their place sterilized as if it were prepped for surgery.

Her hypercritical glare dissected me.

Man, those are the most beautiful eyes. I'm not blind to where they travelled and how her lips parted when I winked back.

And I enjoyed it. What the heck?

I am supposed to fall in love with a down to earth Indian woman who loves to cook, who would encourage me to reapply for university, so I can become that doctor that everyone wanted me to be. I'm supposed to marry someone I can speak sweet Punjabi nothings to, as I massage her back after a long day of hard labour, caring for our flock of little brown children… if she can accept me as is.

Don't get me wrong, I love my grandmother, but she was a nightmare to live with. When Dad lost his job, she was too much. He did what he had to do to provide, but Mom still had to send her *ammi jaan* to the retirement home. It goes against our family's traditional values, but Mom is happier. Dad coped, since she is his air, and he would do anything for her happiness.

Point is, I am not going to waste my time flirting with an uptight, blonde nurse.

Well flirting with intentions. If a suave comment here or there causes her to stumble, I want to be there when she trips. Oh, I want to watch her fall.

I poke my head around the shop.

"Where's Landon?"

"On the phone," Doug says.

Ah. As always. Contacting suppliers seems next to impossible, but I need to know if the natural gas hot water tank is in for the house Juan is working at. His boss finally fired that idiot plumber he'd been using for years and switched to our company; which now means, Juan's sub-trade older brother, me, is going to prove how sub-awesome my work actually is.

It's not. But I can play along and nark on Neil's coworkers. I'm going to enjoy heckling them.

Meeting Landon in his office, he covers his hand over the mouthpiece of the phone. "Hey, you busy?"

I shake my head. "Finished early." Technically I could be. I'm supposed to go to a new build now, but I'd rather start the big job tomorrow.

"Great. One of the main water pipes burst at Clear Valley Trailer Park."

I cuss. "Again?"

He shrugs, returning to his phone call.

Duty calls.

Chapter Six

Hannah

I crouch to the stack of grocery baskets and as I'm reaching to pick one up, I bump into a large hand. My eyes shift up connecting with the stranger's eyes. He is far too pale to be Benji, not that I would ever hope to see his dirty, bearded, pierced-ears face again. It has been a month since he pulled his little forgoing shirt stunt in my apartment, and I couldn't be more relieved he actually did his job satisfactorily.

Fixing the plumbing!

As frustrating as he was, I thankfully may never have to see him again and could perhaps think about another guy for a change, like this one whom I accidentally brushed against… someone put together.

"Oops sorry," I say, feeling ridiculous for being over eager to enter the supermarket. From a quick glance, he has probably recently finished his shift like most people this hour and is in a rush to pick up a gallon of milk and a couple other ingredients for his wife to complete dinner, so she can feed their cranky kids.

"Oh no. I'm sorry. Please." He steps back, offering me to pick up the top basket.

"No. No. It's okay. You go first."

"Ladies first?" His lip curls upward. At another glance, I notice his hand is bare. No ring is tying this man down.

Single? Interesting.

And handsome too, with a white collared buttoned up shirt, grey slacks, gold tie, this man is classy. His dark hair is short, he is clean shaven. Check. Check. Check. He ticks every box on the boyfriend-material list.

I smile up, up, way up to the stranger with the plastic basket in hand. Six feet or taller? Check.

"Thank you. Most people believe chivalry is dead."

"In that case, most people are wrong." He picks up a basket for himself. "I would open the second set of doors for you but they're automatic." Chivalry? Check.

I tap my hair, to ensure the bobby pins are holding my strays in place. "I'm Hannah." I hold out my hand like a blundering fool.

He extends his arm to shake it, business-like and cordial.

Gentle grip. His hands are clean, smooth, and clear from blemish. These hands could model.

Wonderful. Am I imagining things? Is this man for real?

"Aaron."

"Well Aaron, it was lovely meeting you. Unfortunately I have to um, buy groceries."

He smirks. "Me too."

I giggle, proceeding into the store. I unfold my list categorized by food type and fill the basket item by item. In aisle four, I bump into Mr. Wonderful again. "Oh hi again." I bite my lip. "Aaron."

"Hi... Hannah," he says with a sparkle in his eyes. It could be the fluorescent lighting.

"Hey, you shop with a list too!" Somebody pinch me. We have so much in common already.

He glances down to his yellow square note. "It saves money sticking to a plan." Sliding the paper into his pocket, his eyes slant to me. "Did you know that all the staple items are around the perimeter? Bakery, meat, dairy, produce, so if you avoid the middle, you avoid overspending and all the unhealthy stuff."

"We're in the center aisle."

"Yes, well, I can't live without my coffee." He grins, picking up a bag of higher end lightly roasted coffee beans. "Are you a coffee drinker?"

I lift the pre-ground coffee beans from my basket, then plunk them in again. They're generic and on sale. At the quantity I consume it; this is all I can afford. "I live off of this."

"What about dinner?"

"Are you asking me to dinner, or asking if I'm a fan of dinner?"

"I'm asking if you're interested in having dinner with me?" Oh. Me? Aw shucks.

"I'd love to but..."

He glances down.

"No. I mean yes, I'd love to. Only, I have groceries to purchase and... yeah." My sentence falls short. I didn't plan to go on a date when I wrote this grocery list and I have leftovers in the fridge. I pinch my shirt, pulling the collar over my mouth, blushing. How sweet of him.

"Would you like to... tomorrow night?"

"The fact I'm not working tomorrow is in your favour, Aaron. Yes please." We exchange numbers, then he waves goodbye on his way to the express lane with eleven items. The rule is twelve items or less. He may just be Mr. Perfect.

Unfortunately, I'm not as proficient a shopper as him, so I roam through the adjacent aisle for snacks and pre-made curry sauce packets. I scour the shelves. The flavour I like is near the bottom. I scoot beside the stacker's dolly with a wall of product to be shelved. A grey cart blocks my path. Glancing up, my eyes meet Benji with a snide grin. The item I need is right by his heel.

"Peach."

"Mario," I sneer back.

His brows twitch, accepting the acknowledgement as a compliment. It wasn't.

"What are you doing here?"

"Buying food."

"Here? Can't you buy food at the other grocery store?"

"Oh I'm sorry, is this *your* grocery store?" he says, splaying a hand on his chest, feigning offence.

"Just move. You're in the way."

"Can't. Someone's in my way."

"You can back up."

"You could too, but that involves physical effort." My eyes drift to the cart expecting chips, pop, and frozen dinners. Instead I find copious amounts of produce, whole grain products like wild rice, and large slabs of raw meat. So what, the plumber can cook more than boxed macaroni and cheese. Why do I care?

"Celery?" I question with skepticism leaking in my tone as I stare into his cart.

"Are you food shaming me?"

"No. I just... I have never met someone who loves celery."

"With peanut butter it's tolerable." I spot the jar of all-natural, low sodium peanut butter. Almond butter is beside it.

"Why?"

"Because I'm an old man, Hannah. I have to eat healthy or I'll get fat again."

I squint, he seems like all muscle to me.

"You're not that old. We're like what... three years apart, and everyone's metabolism is different." Why did I remember his age? I ask everyone's birthday, literally to hundreds of people every week. Why do I remember his?

"Mine's a lazy..." I scowl at his casual use of profane language. "...So I'm stuck eating rabbit food."

"Well could you tell your lazy *bum* metabolism to move?"

"One sec." He pulls out his phone to text. Not read a text, to text. He hums to the store's background music as he taps away on the cracked screen.

Ugh! Why does he have to be so... Benji! I push the cart into his chest until I can pick up the sauce packet.

"Tikka Masala isn't that difficult to make from scratch. Once you have the real thing, you can't go back. Maybe I'll nab some from my mom's place."

Um... that was weird. "Stealing from your mom? I'll pass. No, thank you."

"It's okay. She has other reasons to hate me. My appreciation for her cooking is probably one of the few things that keep me from being disowned. She always makes extra. It's no biggie."

"Huh." Wow. That is all I can say? First I judge his groceries; next I don't bother to console him when he is in desperate need of a hug. I'm not doing it. He is probably covered in invisible superbug bacteria.

"If not, I could cook some for you. Are you busy tomorrow?"

Why is he… is this the same man from before? Benji is not sugar sweet. He has something nefarious planned under his tattered sleeve.

"Very!" I snap, rushing down the aisles to collect my last two items. Even if Aaron wasn't my knight in shining armour, I would not subject myself to an evening of torture in that plumber's filthy bachelor pad. He wasn't serious, was he? That had to be a joke.

When I arrive at the express lane, the only cashier lane available, Benji and his full cart somehow managed to end up in front of me.

Splendid... not!

He has fabric bags too. Because he is him, and he sees it's me, he takes his sweet time, milking the moment, aligning each item unevenly. Light items mixed with heavy. *No, he's going to crush his fruit! Bah!* Narrow with short. The thin bag flops over spilling in the cart. Benji pauses from his progress to realign it all while chatting with the cashier in a half English, half French conversation.

I'm going to die here… hungry.

Chapter Seven

Benji

Juan and I clock out at 6:30 PM, and that's including the emergency call I woke up to this morning for a broken pipe. I warned the customer, if they wait two hours it would be half the price, but they insisted I arrive at six-freaking AM. Who's up that early? Me.

"I'm taking you to dinner."

Juan gives me a quizzical glance. Mom's cooking is great and all, but my brother has no social life outside of the workplace.

We seat ourselves at a local family restaurant. Great atmosphere. The tables are cheap, but they try to fancy them up with vinyl cloths. Families of all shapes and sizes fill these tables. I like the place because they put enough food on the plate without robbing my bank account. Before my diet, I ate here often… hence the diet.

"Aren't you on a diet?"

"Screw the diet. I need a burger."

The waitress tucks her loose lock of hair behind her ear, eyeing up the both of us, deciding who to greet first. Juan wins, but I'm first to order.

"Coffee. Deluxe burger. Extra everything." The waitress knows me well enough, she doesn't bother for clarification. Even with peanut butter, I can't stand celery. They're like mutant blades of grass. No, grass would taste better. Celery has no taste, yet it also has no calories. I am too close to give up now. I'll run an extra two kilometres tonight for this, but it will be worth it.

"One Benji burger coming right up. And for you, fine fellow?"

Juan purses his lips with his usual cold and aloof expression, skimming through the menu. "Water. The Schnitzel club, I guess."

We hand our menus to the waitress.

"Hey, it's that hot nurse chick." Juan jerks his head to one of the many tables behind me.

"Ha. Funny."

"No, I'm serious."

I twist, perking an eyebrow in disbelief once I've confirmed it's her. I don't turn back. Idiotically, I study her, from her white heels, up her slender calves to her angelic summer dress.

"Hmm... peachy." Again with the lace.

Mumbling to myself, I can't help but bite my lip, admiring her straight hair braided to the side. What happened to the perfectly centered, perfectly balanced, perfectly pinned back cheerleader hairstyle… the one that swung pom-poms in my chest?

Why braids?

I love braids, the way each strand intertwines with the other. I'm at a loss to whether I would stroke it, stare, or stick my fingers through to mess it up. With each weave I realize the hair over her scalp is brighter than the strands behind her all-natural golden blonde. Her date can't appreciate it from his view, yet he tilts his head to the side when he catches Juan and I gawking at them. Her tall, dark-haired, white guy, without an ounce of legitimate muscle, is clean shaven, and has a pristine white shirt that's actually white… like it could glow in sunlight—bleach commercial white. And no surprise, he wears khaki pants like a boring prude.

An expensive looking stainless steel pen pokes out his shirt pocket. I glance down to my Leatherman and permanent markers covered in something.

"How's Jenny?" I change the subject, anything but them.

The waitress returns with our drinks. Juan sips into his ice cold water without a nod or smile of appreciation. "She's returning to school in the fall, so we mutually broke up." The napkin underneath folds up, giving me a quick glimpse of the waitress' phone number.

"That's it?"

"Meh." He plays with his ice cubes. Threading them onto his straw and balancing them before he slides them back into the glass.

"Was she a bad kisser?" What he seeks in a woman is shallow and predictable, but with looks like his, he can get away with it.

"I didn't bother."

Huh, and Mom is somehow concerned about me.

"Hey Benji, why's that nurse with that noob instead of you?"

"I told you I'm not into Hannah."

"Hmm. Sure, whatever."

Curious, I peek back at Hannah's date. He's treating her to dessert, separate plates. "Yeah, even if I was, that's not going anywhere." I gesture to them with my thumb. "If he's playing for keeps he should know to always share the dessert." Dang, what I'd do to smear that peach cobbler onto her face right now, then I'd find any excuse to wipe it off her cheek, lips. There'd be a dollop of whipped cream bopped on the nose and I'd have to resort to a fun peck to clean her off. Maybe I would have reserved a private booth so the tykes wouldn't grimace. Hannah and a private booth, what an intriguing concept. Her beauty could erase bits of my prejudice.

Nah. This is Hannah, the trigger happy—correction—needle-jab happy, nurse.

Juan crosses his arms over his broad chest. It's challenging to take him seriously, when I remember when he was only waist high. He can try, but he won't intimidate me.

"I'm not taking dating advice from a celibate bachelor."

His loss.

Someone taps my shoulder. Glancing up, Hannah and her pretty-boy wave at us.

I stumble, nearly falling out of my chair. Gripping onto the table saves me. What the crap, he's tall, like almost as tall as Neil's newest apprentice, Reagan. Holding onto my chest, I focus on steadying my breathing until my heart rate is under control. It would help if she stopped searching for my eyes.

I don't want to do anything more stupid. *Please don't look at me, especially like that.*

"Hi Benji. This is Aaron..."

Juan giggles into his fist. Ugh. My brother is so flipping immature. Hannah links her arm with this Aaron weirdo.

"...my boyfriend. Isn't he perfect?"

Hannah has her makeup to a minimum, neat and tidy, just like her. Lip gloss and mascara, but it's still twisting my gut into knots. Is that glitter on her cheeks? Her side swept bangs are tucked back with a matching butterfly clip. Bah! Could she be any girlier? Her look is bringing me back to my high school days. Somehow she pulls it off, and is un-freaking-believably adorable.

I nod as if I don't care.

"He's an accountant."

Ooh, how exhilarating! Now I cover my fist over my mouth, holding in a chuckle. Realizing I have to say something, I mumble, "Cool. Does he have herpes too?"

Her mouth gapes.

I'm sorry. I had to! I couldn't resist, and the risk paid off. Her face is beet red. Aaron's eyes go wide, repulsed, shifting between Hannah and I for answers.

"No, this isn't my boyfriend," I add for clarification. "This is my brother Juan. Howdy." If I were to be gay, which I'm not, so straight or gay, I wouldn't be with a guy, person, whatever ten years younger than me. That's a decade, a whole generation of common ground poof—gone. Just not my thing. Juan tips an imaginary cowboy hat.

Hannah's fists clench to the point her nails are digging into her skin. "Stop bringing it up!"

"He can't." Juan cuts in. "You uh... bring it out." Chuckling he adds, "Shooting him with all sorts of ideas. The dress, the sass, the—" I glare at him to shut up. There is no reason for my junk to enter this discussion, especially if he's bang on. "The word that rhymes." He waggles his brows, but I swear that innocent blush of hers has transformed into blood curdling wrath. Her face is so red, I'm milliseconds from her fist in my face.

She's too civil to punch, but as a medic she holds ulterior methods to my demise.

"I'm sorry, okay. It was a mistake." Hannah turns to her boyfriend, sliding her hand behind her neck, with an expression of uneasiness.

"What happened?" Aaron glances down to her beady blue eyes.

She scowls. "I'm legally not supposed to tell you."

Patient confidentiality. Juan and I grin at each other like we discovered the forbidden red button. He knows the story, I had to spill.

"Anyways, we have to go. Aaron here... is taking me to a movie." Her tone perplexes me, as if she's asking for my permission. Last time I checked, not that I actually did check, but from what I remember she definitely wore big girl panties. I'm sure she will survive.

I glance down at my coffee. Did someone spike this too?

"Hmm. Romantic." I roll my eyes. Yes, take the prettiest girl in the whole world into a dark room, where he will instead stare at a massive screen. He's too square for any twisted motives. If it were me, after a shower, and with a clean-ish shirt, and she being dressed like that, I'd take her to the drop-in couple's night at the dance studio. I can't remember if they do swing or ballroom, but what woman wouldn't find dancing as an enchanting date? That is, if she would trust me and let me take the lead. If it's too public for her tastes, we could go to one of the parks and I'd play something off my phone. "Have fun you two."

They pay the waitress then leave the restaurant.

Our food arrives. The waitress' gaze lingers on Juan. He grins back courteously,

"There was not an ounce of chemistry between them, eh?"

"Not a drop." I confirm, biting in a burning hot potato fry. "You up for a movie?"

"Not really." Juan lowers his sandwich. "So... tell me about celibacy."

"I'm not..." I squirt ketchup on my plate. "I can't date her."

"You can't or won't? Because won't implies you're choosing not to."

"*Can't* implies I can't take her off my mind, because something's holding me back. I barely know her. I don't need you reminding me fifty times a day how attractive she is. The plumbing is well aware. Things are just different with me than they are for you. I have baggage."

"You've lost weight."

"Not that type of baggage, you dip..." I mute myself from cursing in a restaurant.

"But you want to date her."

"Can't! Plus she has a boyfriend and she hates my guts, so it's no big deal."

Chapter Eight

Hannah

Dinners, movies, strolling downtown, dating Aaron has been fun, I guess. Unfortunately, that isn't most days. I work most Saturdays and my graveyard shifts take a toll on him. My new boyfriend's schedule is steady: Monday to Friday, nine to four. It's easy to remember. Steady.

Mine is four tens day-shift, one day off, three nights on, two days off, another set of nights, five actually, and it is always changing. Then sometimes I have to swap shifts if someone is sick or is on holiday. Not to mention the hospital does not close for statutory holidays, so Aaron isn't necessarily terrible at keeping up to my pace.

Last week was the first time I wore heels in over a year. I live in runners and scrubs. I have on occasion passed out on the couch from exhaustion before making it to my bed.

This dating gig feels a lot harder than it should be. I thought it would come naturally, being with someone so similar and sweet, but if I had to be honest, I think I'm not fitting in. It's cute that he tries. I wish I could pinpoint it, but it feels like even though he checks off my list, I don't check off his. I don't know who that person is, but I'd rather be me.

Today our schedules lined up, so after my shift and on his day off, Aaron insisted we play a board game. He spent the first hour explaining the rules to me and I still haven't grasped the concept. There are levels, currency, armour, and multiple decks. It is a lot to soak in and my brain is fried.

Our pieces line up perfectly along the board, something we can agree on, but I am bored out of my mind.

A token knocks over. We rush to fix it, bumping hands, however before I'm able to appreciate the contact he shouts, "Ha! Beat you to it."

Yeah, neat.

His home is beautiful: clean, modern, cookie-cutter. I sigh, resting my face into my palm. He's so put-together. All the books on his shelves are lined up aesthetically in their genre group and with decorative bookends. The movies are alphabetized. His shoes are on the shoe racks. I wonder if he paid for all of this by himself or if he comes from a rich family. I've never been in a home that looks like it was pulled out of a current magazine. Every little thing has a place and it actually is where it's supposed to be, like a hotel lobby. Plus his infuser makes the room smell like jasmine.

"Hannah, you're adorable."

I smile at his kind words. This should make my heart flutter, how he only looks into my eyes, never wandering his gaze, never changing his tone to test me, and never blurting rude comments causing me to imagine scenarios I shouldn't. I guess this is how taking it slow feels.

"You're not in the mood, are you?"

Mood?

"The gaming mood."

Oh. Not really. I shake my head agreeing with him.

Aaron is sweet. He is Mr. Perfect. He has the right words to say, he holds to integrity, carrying it out in his occupation, and he is organized. He plans our dates ahead of time, being extra flexible for me—thoughtful.

Only the silence between us seems too eerie.

Nevertheless, it trumps and will always trump seeing Benjamin Gakhar. Who does he think he is, entering a restaurant with mud to his calves then silently judging who I choose to date? I barely know the idiot. Ugh, tradesmen, they're all the same. They catcall any woman strolling down the street. No standards.

Plumbers are the worst. I swear every piece of equipment, every phrase is a dirty innuendo. And his intense glare, I don't dare consider what's tinkering in that empty head of his. Is there any word in that small brain of his that contains more than four letters?

He probably is a worse kisser than Aaron, and lives in a house full of belching belly button picking bachelors. Who would want his rough scruff to scrape their face anyway?

It's probably super poky. They would have to try really hard to feel the softness of those lips. Oh, and I bet he has an I-heart-Mom tattoo on his big round gluteus maximus.

My mind drifts, reminded of silly details like how he wore brand name briefs, or how his muscles would clench and flex as he fixed my drains… in the apartment. The actual drains not the… forget it. Smiling as he worked a sweat. Not that I recall his visit from over a month ago when he did his job, one that he is paid to do. Yeah, there's nothing sexy about a man who is paid to plunge toilets.

Hard earned muscles, no brain… no thank you.

And his 'witty' comebacks? So annoying. Ugh! Why does he make it his job to frustrate me? Can't he let it go? I messed up one time, and it had to be with him. The breakup, losing a patient, then meeting him. I wasn't professional, and I wish he wouldn't remind me of a shift I'll always regret. In my line of work a mistake could cost a life, instead it is costing my social reputation.

"Maybe I should get going." I shouldn't, but we're going nowhere. Aaron is supposed to help me forget that man. Instead, I'm replaying the shock on Benji's face when he saw me in one of my favourite dresses. This is the third date I've left nearly an hour earlier than planned. Perhaps it's my exhaustion, or the eerie sense I've been lingering too long, as in I've socialized enough for one day and want to curl into my covers and be a hermit for the rest of the evening.

Aaron stands, helping me to the door.

Maybe I should end it. He hasn't done anything wrong, and what am I supposed to say? It's not fair I have someone else on my mind.

Aaron stares down at my face. His hand shakes. Is he always going to be a ball of nervous energy? Am I?

I gulp.

"Uh..." He dips to press his lips against mine, too soft, too quick, too calculated and by the book. It's foreign, no... bizarre—lacking any trace of intimate emotion. "Goodnight."

I must be out of it. This is my fault. I'm not in the mood, but when will I be? When do the butterflies break from their cocoon? My heart is feeling a little dusty. Maybe I'm not ready for a long-term relationship, or any. Except our relationship is young, I should give Aaron the benefit of the doubt. What was he initially attracted to, because he isn't showing any clues. Maybe it's his set of boundaries. I feel like there's a thick line dividing us, and we're not going to cross it any time soon, as if he's too cordial.

No. I wanted this.

It must be his sense of order. To me that reads as reliable. He is a list person. He has high standards which explains why he is so perfect; it makes me want to be a better person too. I relate. There are no bitter surprises with him. Beyond that, I suppose we'll find out.

We will just have to take it nice and slow. Painfully slow.

It was fairly quiet during my shift tonight—last night, yesterday, whatever—at the hospital. No one was hit by a car or had their appendix explode, a real treat. I kept thinking about Aaron and me and we're really that. His kiss didn't pull me in, which doesn't make sense. He is a good man, attractive and kind. The pieces should all fit together, but they just won't.

I stare out to the sunrise as I approach my car. What day of the week is it again? I crash into the vinyl seat and jam my key into the ignition. I'll figure it out when I wake up from my much-needed slumber. I have literally clocked out in more ways than one, so if I can get home in one piece, that would be more than enough.

Pitta-tta-tah-tuh

I groan. Please no. Not now.

Pitta-tta-tah-tuh

Whipping out my phone from my purse, I call Aaron. Not my roommate. That would be useless considering she's never around and probably knows less about vehicles than me. However, since my boyfriend sets his texts to vibrate, he wouldn't hear the beeps if I tried.

"Hmm? Hannah? What..." I imagine him rubbing his eyes, stretching his face with a flat palm. "Is everything alright?"

I sigh, yawning in the process. "I'm sorry for waking you up. I need your help."

"At this hour?" He could grumble, but his tone is sparing. "What would you need help with at five in the morning?"

"My car won't start. Could you jump it?"

"I uh... I don't know how." I hear his anxious swallow. "Do you want me to call a mechanic, or pick you up?" Anything but a mechanic. Living in this small town, I'd be bound to bump into a peculiar one. Not happening. Nope.

I scratch my forehead. The hairs loosen from my ponytail and fall into my eyes.

"Don't worry. I'll call one of my buddies." We end the call on good terms. I skim through my contact list, surprised my ex-boyfriend is still there.

Not happening.

Sighing again, I contemplate who else I know who's good at fixing things.

Benji.

Not him either! I snarl at the idea of him finding an excuse to peel his shirt to do the job. Something like clean off the oil of his wrench. Why did he have to meticulously stare at me on my date? It wasn't with him. Ha! He can dream on. Why would I want it to be with a man who thinks it is socially acceptable to eat at a restaurant in his filthy gear? I am not being ridiculous. The poor waitress must have spent hours mopping up his muddy boot prints after his meal. Why didn't it bother him? I'm with the perfect guy—his opposite.

Why couldn't Aaron intimidate him?

Ugh! His cool and collected composure, it infuriates me. Doesn't Benji have anything better to do than glare at me in ways that get inside my head? He is not my type and there has to be someone around here I've befriended that can fix my car.

Somebody. Anybody else.

I open my wallet calculating whether or not I could afford a different mechanic, or tow truck, but instead I find Benji's white business card with an oily thumbprint. The thought of sanitizing my hands runs through my mind. Somehow, I'm convinced he'd do the favour for free, if it meant he could tease me. A few harsh words are worth a free repair, especially since my nursing textbooks cost thousands of dollars, an expense I am still paying off.

Debt can make a woman desperate.

I hold the ringing phone to my ear. *You can do this.*

"Good morning, princess."

I open my mouth, but he cuts me off.

"Need me to flush your pipes?"

"You did not!" Benji did not just spout a sexual innuendo off the fly. Ugh. Disgusting!

He chuckles. "What? It's how I answer all my calls."

"Right, and somehow I'm supposed to believe that?"

"Okay fine, Princess Peach, it's how I answer calls at bloody freaking 5:10 AM. What the heck woman, did your roommate flush the whole flipping tampon box in one go? It's been like a month."

"It's my car."

His mocking laughter fills the other end. "Let me get this straight. You're calling the plumber to fix your car? Maybe you should call a carpenter to tighten those loose screws." Is he wiping a tear from his eye? This was a mistake.

"Ha. Ha. Please Benji," I beg. I am not proud of my whining tone.

"Say it again."

"Please." Deadpan. I am so not in the mood.

"More squeal. I need you to cry out my name, like you would normally this late in the night, morning... whatever time you would."

"You're disgusting."

"Maybe you don't need my help." Is he picking at his dirt encrusted fingernails?

I growl.

"Close enough. What's wrong with your car?"

"It won't start."

"Your car or your boyfriend? Hey where is that boyfriend of yours anyways? Can't he help?"

"He doesn't know how."

"He doesn't know how to connect one battery to another? Sheesh, Hannah. I don't know. Sounds like you got yourself a girlfriend." Wow. I can't believe he went there. In this day in age anybody can be anybody, like how he can be this exasperating instead of charming.

"That's incredibly sexist. Men don't have to be good with tools."

"No, but that would be your loss, now wouldn't it?"

Alone in the parking lot my cheeks flush with heat. I tug on the neckline of my scrub top and waft it around to cool down.

"Will you help me? Can you jump it?"

"Define 'it.'"

"You are unbelievable." On second thought. I regret this. Why do I even bother?

"Oh princess, wouldn't you like to find out."

Again, I grunt. This is so not the time. I'm exhausted. I want to go home and shower off all this bacteria and Benji's comments if possible.

"I'm at the hospital. Can you come now?"

"Dang and you're calling me the dirty one. Well aren't you a little demanding. One sec, I'm with my boyfriend. I'll be there shortly."

"Just to be clear, you don't have a boyfriend..." Or girlfriend with his grouchy attitude.

"If that's the lie you tell yourself to be with your pretty-boy then what if I do?"

"You don't."

"No..." he cusses. And here we almost lasted a full conversation without him mucking it up.

"Stop swearing!"

"Stop hurting my feelings."

I hang up. Benjamin Gakhar is ridiculous! That man doesn't have feelings. He is as thick skinned as they get… a crude craftsman at most. If he's going to play like that, he should understand the more vile he gets, the more vicious I become.

I fix my makeup in the mirror as I wait, capping my lip gloss when I spot him stepping out a hemi engine truck with mud streaks on the side. The last thing I need is to look haggard from my graveyard shift, especially in front of him. Benji arrived promptly within ten minutes in a purple graphic T-shirt, shorts, and leather sandals. Sunglasses hang off his shirt to add to his relaxed vibe. I read his shirt.

You done messed up A-A-Ron?

Wow, subtle.

He swings the jumper cables like a weighted rope. "Pop the lid, will ya, Blondie?"

I crouch down, searching for the button.

Uh-oh. What does the symbol look like again? He opens the door and finds it in two seconds, returns to the hood, propping it up with the stand, and attaches the clips to both batteries while his truck idles.

I hop out to watch the process, so between Aaron and I, one of us will figure this out for next time, if there is one.

"I'm surprised you didn't ask one of your coworkers to help you out."

I glance around to a semi full staff parking lot then smack my forehead. Stupid tired brain! He is right for once. Literally anyone, maybe not in emergency, but anybody could have helped me out.

"Hey." He pats my shoulder. "I don't mind."

I give him an incredulous stare.

"I will when I start work in two hours and the coffee needs a boost." He waits for my smile, I'm still glaring. "So... Aaron, the girlfriend, isn't much of a handyman, eh?"

I cross my arms. "No. He's brilliant with numbers."

Benji lifts an eyebrow, "And you're into that?"

"Can't land up in the ER using an adding machine, now can you?" I sigh, feeling the need to fix my hair, but resist. He stares at the ground briefly with his hands in his pockets. "Sorry," I apologize, realizing I've mistakenly been using that snippy tone with him. He didn't report me when I had my worst of days, so he isn't necessarily the worst human being to exist.

He answered the phone. He is here when he doesn't have to be. Plus he has put up with me this far. There aren't many people who would drive out this early to deal with my car woes, but he is still a cussing plumber.

Again, he raises his eyebrow, this time with an easy-going smirk.

"Sorry for misdiagnosing you to have herpes." I clarify, "Could you stop with the jokes now? They're not funny."

"Nah."

I stomp my sneaker foot on the pavement. "I'm serious! I don't like to make mistakes and I certainly don't like them wafted in my face, reminding me of the one time I fell short."

His lips part. "Everyone makes mistakes."

"Except in my line of work, a mistake could cost someone's life… and that's on me."

Chapter Nine

Benji

A mistake could cost someone their life. I live with that guilt every day of my own life. Now that she brings that up, the flirty game is over. I lose. Hannah is happy with her over-dependant prissy boyfriend and I'm hitting on someone who is taken.

"Benji?"

"Hmm?" I take a deep breath, returning to her glassy blue eyes. I've seen the shade a million times, yet on her, the aqua tint may never fail to intrigue me. This is the part where I say something encouraging so I'm not a complete dirtbag, and she won't view me as the hypocrite that I am.

"You can't let the little mishaps eat at you." I hold out my hands to hers. They're clean but marred from drill bits, screws, torch burns, knife cuts—name it and I've got it. "You know, I've never seen you with your hair down, literally and figuratively," I tell her. *Also I excelled in high school calculus.* It was one of my favourite subjects. I keep that last bit to myself, not that she'll believe me, but if she's really into numbers... forget it.

Hannah flicks her ponytail, pretending she's unaffected by my words, but her eyes speak for themselves as the gateway to her mind.

"You uh... have these problems often with your car?"

She tightens her hair elastic, rubs her eyes, and lets out a sigh of exhaustion. "Little things here and there. I currently can't afford to change vehicles, maybe a repair but..."

"But?" I lean closer. My hip bumps hers. She crosses her arms again, disgruntled. There's a story she is hiding, and I have to prod out. "You have something against mechanics too?"

"Just one."

She can chew her lip all she wants, I'm not leaving until she spits out a name.

"Mack."

Oh him. "Yeah, he's a huge—"

Her scowl mutes me. She relaxes, revealing a faint smile, and that one action triples the size of my ego or at least gets my heart racing.

"Let me guess, he cheated on you?"

"No. Mack never did."

Oh he did, only she never found out. Mack always has a second option, a plan B, C, D, E, F, and G.

"He just… don't judge me, okay? I was new to town, I didn't know anybody and... yep, I'm leaving it there."

"Nah. Keep going. Stories at five AM are the best kind."

"Fine. He was accident prone. Saw the reckless idiot more in the ER than I did for a date. Watching a man's arms flex while they work is one thing, but taping on a cast is another."

I knew it. A fist pump would be too obvious, so I keep the excitement to myself. What girl can resist a man with well earned grease stains? But this new intel on arms… they're my only feature until I can burn off the remaining ten pounds since the incident.

"And now you assume all blue-collars are reckless idiots who always injure themselves." I point to the scar on my thumb. It healed... as well as it could considering the crap I put my stitches through, both literally and figuratively. "We're not. Some of us use our brains on the jobsite, but on occasion accidents happen. People make mistakes, but we heal. We move on."

Or we don't.

Then we wallow in guilt, and we wish we could turn back the clock and prevent it all, reverse the gamble, and avoid the thrill.

Giving advice is always easier than applying it. However, maybe this conversation is spurring in me to accept the bitter pill and swallow. And dang it, who else is better to administer the medication than the smoking hot nurse from the ER?

"Let's try to start your car now." With a twist of her wrist, the key activates the vehicle. Her engine while it may not purr, it runs.

I remove the cables swiftly, push down the hood, and give her car a gentle pat. With the sun up, I flick on my shades, and pivot on my heel, returning to my truck when her high-pitched voice halts me.

"Thank you."

I should leave before she rips the Band-Aid.

I should move my feet.

I should, shouldn't I?

Staring down at my T-shirt I whisper, "You're welcome." Man, I must be a total jerk. Juan and I thought it would be funny to wear this around her. This Aaron guy is lucky. I shouldn't be this greedy jealous type. Over a month ago, I was content living as a bachelor for the rest of my life. I thought I grew out of crushing on cute girls. But none of them have been as cute as her. No other woman has crawled under my skin, irritated me, and remained this adorable. He probably likes that about her too. I'm not going to break them up.

Even if I want her.

Even if I don't want to leave this dumb hospital parking lot, only because she's five feet behind me and we need to vent: her and her ex, me and my life's collection of craptastic moments. Real talk. Tough love. After all her spiteful greetings, she might be tolerable. Heck, relatable.

No. Plunge that crud deeper. I'm not sharing, not with her.

I wave back and clear my throat, deepening my voice in the process.

"Aaron's a cool guy. I didn't mean what I said."

"Good."

My jaw drops. *Good?* Her tone. Sheesh! It's so petty. Like "of course he's a good guy, Benji, you're an idiot to not see it," *good.* I clench my fists and drive off, roaring the hemi engine of my truck through the sleeping neighbourhoods. If only I could leave her in a cloud of black smoke.

"Your phone's ringing," Justin says, as I muster all my strength, dripping in sweat head to toe to stretch the flexible PVC coupling over the pre-existing copper drain. It's connection after connection with little give. If I screw this up, we're replacing the whole piece.

"I can't answer."

"It's your mom."

"I'll call her back." My fingers are slipping. I cuss profusely "It's so tight. Stretch wider for me." I talk to the pipe as if it's listening, like it could somehow help the situation, "Open up for me! Agh!" My arms shake.

"Really man, do you listen to yourself?"

I tell him to shut up in the least respectable manner. I'm doing my job; he doesn't have to be a pervert about it. The black rubber coupling slaps over the copper pipe rim. I gasp with relief, taking a full minute to catch my breath. Holding out an open palm, Justin plunks my phone onto my slimy hand.

I listen to my voicemail.

"Benjamin, it is your mother. Come to the house, immediately. It is important." That's it. Not, 'Hey son. How are you?' Could she perhaps share what is in dire need of my attention? I'm at work. Can it wait? Did something break down? Is Juan out of town today? Could she not reach him? Why didn't Dad call? If Mom wants to talk to me, she does so through Juan.

Something is up.

The moment I clock out, I skip the company chit-chat and drive straight to my parents' house on Maple Street. The bees buzz happily in and out of the blooms. With a heavy exhale, I lift my fist to the wooden door.

"*Sat sri akal!*" I say with a wide grin plastered on my face to elevate the mood. One can never tell with her constant disapproving tone. "What broke?" I didn't bother switching vehicles despite my house being closer to the shop than theirs. My toolbag is in the back of my work van, although I can't see what could be so challenging that even *widdle* Juan couldn't fix.

"Nothing," Mom shouts from down the hall. She rushes over to me in hurried tip-toed steps, giving me a warm welcoming hug, extending it for longer than usual. "Sit, sit. I made you tea." She crosses her legs as she seats herself on the cushioned rocking chair she reupholstered in a floral fabric.

"Tea?" I tilt my head to the side. *What the words-my-mother-should-never-hear-me-say!* She repeats herself, this time with a stern glare.

Okay, tea it is.

She pours chai into two gold-rimmed china cups. I sit on the couch with my back straight, shoulders back. She hands me mine, with the matching saucer underneath. Even Dad, intimidated by her presence, decides he doesn't actually want to wheel into the living room. The way he reaches over for his book with his lips zipped shut to wheel backwards into the master suite speaks volumes.

"Benjamin." Mom's lips hover over the rim of her teacup.

"Benji," I correct, staring at the tea on my lap, weirded out by the floral dish over my canvas pants. I like to be called Benji. Benjamin is too official.

"Benjamin," her authoritative tone doubles. What did I do this time to deserve this interrogation?

"Yes, Mom?" I sip the tea, with my pinkie high just to agitate her. Hey, if she isn't going to call me Benji, two can play at this game.

"You are turning thirty soon."

Yes? You gave birth to me. I am aware you are aware of this fact, Mom. I take another sip. Her lips press into a firmer line staring at my pinkie. The china teacup is smaller than my hands. Pinch too hard and I could crack the handle off. I choose to hold it up, but my finger curls as my own version of a dog having its tail between its legs.

"Yep. The big three-zero. We'll have to have a big party. Something rowdy... a shindig perhaps. I'm thinking a barbeque at my—"

Mom cuts me off abruptly, standing on her toes. "Benjamin Gakhar! You're single... at thirty!"

I gulp down the rest of my tea, burning my mouth. Thirty's not that old in the dating world these days. As I'm figuratively pinching my mouth shut from shouting nasty words, her dark eyes flood with disappointment.

More disappointment.

I moved out.

I ditched the culture.

I chose the apprenticeship over more school.

I don't have the prestigious job she wanted for me.

"Dad married me when he was twenty-one!"

This isn't anything new, yet out of all the things I have or have not done, this hurts her the most. She presses her ankle length skirt flat, returning to her seat. "Our cousins overseas agreed to help. We want to find you a commendable bride."

"What!" I roar. "A what?"

"I want grandkids, someday… while I'm still alive."

"Mom," I groan like a nine-year-old boy. "It's not like I'm your only child."

"Yes, but you're our only one who doesn't try. You haven't even been on a date, let alone asked a girl out. My dear Benjamin, you need a wife. You should move back home. Get married. Return to your roots."

"Mom! I don't need a wife or a girlfriend." And my love life is none of her concern. I think I flirt plenty, as of late, and I'm content with just that. There's no one to impress, no important dates to remember, an entire bed to myself. It's a cushy life. I'm perfectly content with the friends I have made. I like the extra space.

"But you're terribly lonely."

"Mom! I'm not lonely. I have tons of friends. If anyone's a loner it's Juan." He's the one who doesn't try. Girls throw themselves at him like bugs on a windshield.

"I have a life, an established career, a home, vehicle, funds to travel..." Maybe I should travel. The only woman I feel comfortable sharing myself with wants nothing to do with me, because of the most entitled prejudice. Yeah, travel sounds just dandy. "I don't need you to arrange a marriage. We're in North America and it's the twenty-first century. This is my country! I don't want an Indian wife, okay? Not that there's anything wrong with..." I sigh, wiping my face. "I'm not a traditional guy." Heck, Doug and I played Frisbee with a cracked toilet seat on Thursday. Acting like a maharajah or whatever I'm supposed to be in a white town is low on my priority list. I'm not royalty. I'm far from it.

"Your aunts are starting to ask if you're not attracted to women."

"What the..." I tame my tongue for my mother's sake. "I am." There's this opinionated dumb blonde I haven't been able to get out of my head for weeks. She's a career-driven woman, the exact opposite to what mom would approve of.

Good, she says. *Good*. I replay it in my mind, how she went from an adorable *thank you* to *good*.

"Benjamin, listen. Your job might be... less admirable, but the idea of moving here might be convincing enough for her." Yes, a small town in northern Canada surrounded by white people and snow for nine of the twelve month year. "You're a handsome man, it would be a waste to not..."

I shake my head. "You're freaking unbelievable." Only I didn't say freaking.

"You owe me!"

I storm out, slamming the door. The windows rattle. I will not be her puppet.

A commendable bride. She must be out of her bloody mind.

In the evening, I run an extra mile during my workout to clear my head.

It doesn't.

When Monday rolls around, I'm sent out to the white picket fence neighbourhood to fix or possibly replace a bathroom faucet.

Aaron answers his door.

Hmm, just my luck, because I needed one more prompt to keep that nurse in my head.

"Oh hi. You're Hannah's friend." If I'm considered her friend, she doesn't have many. I suppose she doesn't hate me as much as I thought.

"Yeah?" I roll with it. I'm here to fix something, not for pleasantries.

"The faucet isn't working."

"Which one?"

He leads me to the kitchen sink where at full blast it dribbles. I remove the aerator, give it a scrub and save him the hundred dollars, charge him a hundred for my time. Not that I'm trying to stereotype the guy, but he really doesn't have a backbone. His face turned pale when I showed him the scum collected around the piece. Town water is hard, this is normal.

She is a nurse for the emergency room, as in the place where people go when they're bleeding out to death or eat too many laundry pods. I'm almost tempted to remind him that she has to inspect areas of the body he needs to be comparable in. And she has high standards.

Aaron closes his magazine. He winces at a minor paper cut, rushing to the repaired faucet to wash it. He dabs it with rubbing alcohol, and wraps it in a Band-Aid.

I can't see what Hannah finds attractive in him. How many dumb pickup lines do I have to spout until it soaks into her mind sponge? I am heterosexual. I find her very sexually appealing. Her body makes my body react primitively.

Does she really want to spend her off-hours with mister 'lives according to the checklist?' What a waste! People who pay others to do all the work for them make me sick... with pity. It's one thing to hire out someone because of a tight deadline, or if they genuinely need help, but to not try?

Sad.

Those lean muscles he has are from the gym, but they're not impressive. He's not fat, nor does it appear he ever has been, lucky dude. We've bumped paths a few times on Men's Night. He runs the treadmill almost the entire night. If all I was going to do was run, I'd—*I don't know*—maybe go for a run outside while the weather is amazing. Over the past year, I've discovered a few stunning trails.

He'd make a decent friend, sure, but he's so... boring. I sigh, reminded of how Hannah practically worships him. I don't want to bother, but if he really is that important to her... Friends it is.

"Hey uh, I'm having a barbeque this weekend. You and Hannah want to come by?" I offer.

Aaron's ears perk up.

Yeah, I want to see her, not you. Prove to Juan, that Hannah and I will only be friends, and that I accept them. Juan doesn't believe me.

I need to believe it.

Even if there is attraction from both parties, we couldn't base a relationship on just that. We want different things. Hannah wants Mr. Perfect here. And I want to get by in life, the least dramatic way possible. If I were to settle down, which I won't, I would find a homebody to have those grandkids my mom is begging me for.

Being friends means I can keep my distance and I stamp out this silly crush. If she's trying to make me jealous, it's working, unless she's serious about settling for a Mr. Perfect. If that's the case, I'm not the guy she has in her set mind. I never will be. Will that ever change? Could I return to the life I had before I met Hannah, where she wouldn't irk me with her standard of actually caring about every little meaningless thing?

Before I became fascinated with how she overreacts to the simplest phrases, and how relatable and unintentionally down to earth she is.

"Should I bring anything?" Aaron asks.

I gather my tools, regretting this invitation already.

"Chips? I don't know." *Your girlfriend, who is clearly only dating you to prove a point against me.* One in which she is horribly wrong.

"Let me get this straight. You invited Aaron to this barbeque so you could steal his girlfriend," Juan says, flipping the burger patties in my backyard. He is the man of the grill.

"No."

"Then why?" Flip.

"Because I make friends, dimwit. Something you should try."

"I can make friends, I just don't."

I should smack him. Clearly Mother never spanked him hard enough. "Yeah, because you'd rather work overtime."

"I'm saving up for a house. Working for Neil has been great. Benefits, good pay. I think I'll stay with him after the apprenticeship is over."

"You're what?"

"Staying at JRCC."

"Back up a bit. Did you say a house?"

"Yeah Benji, I'm moving out too."

My mouth gapes. "Is Mom okay with that?" Mom was furious when I left, but I couldn't live under the same roof as Dad when what happened, happened. If it wasn't for our parents loving nature, Mom would have disowned me by now. I'm sure by next weekend she'll drop the whole arranged marriage scheme, realizing I'm a hopeless cause, too rebellious for a cure. I get that she cares about these things, but I don't.

"She will have to be," Juan says confidently. "If not, I'll flip it and sell it for twice the price."

I change the subject since Juan is clearly delusional that Mom would let her baby move on and without a wife. "You heard she's trying to set me up?"

Juan chuckles. "Yeah. Did she send you their profiles?"

I grimace while opening the email app on my phone to show him.

"Are these actually the two girls she's been considering?" I ask him.

"They're cute in their pictures," he says optimistically.

I roll my eyes. He is full of it.

"Aarsi Goel and Pooja Khan... Juan, I'm a plumber. I can't marry a girl named Aarsi. The flack the guys would give!"

"What about Hanaya?"

My slit eyes glare up to him. "She's fifteen." I cuss. I don't care if Mom says she is lying about her age, that's gross. How does she expect me to have a fulfilling relationship with any of these kids? "All the girls on Mom's list are under twenty. Even if they were ridiculously stunning and fun and whatever... I'm not marrying a little girl." I pretend to vomit all over our shoes. "That's disgusting and I'm sure it has to be illegal or it should be. I mean, that would be like me taking that high schooler that answers the phone for your boss, what's her name..." I snap my fingers a few times. "Simone... out for a date."

"Aw sweet! Mom brought her mango salsa." Juan wanders off handing me the flipper.

I lost his attention.

Wait, what? I want some! He better save some for me. This is my birthday; I'm not supposed to man the grill. I glance in their direction, noticing Mom readjusting the placement of the large fruit bowl while gabbing to Hannah and like twenty other of my friends congregated around her.

She actually showed up.

And oh no, she's talking to my mom. I need to save her now.

"Hey! Grab me some, will ya?" I holler.

Hannah turns to me, simultaneously hooking her arm with Aaron… defensively. She clings tightly to his side and my stomach twists. I see right through her dumb game. Why does she do this to herself? How long is she going to keep this going?

How do I know this?

Hanging off her wrist is a small gift bag with the tissue paper poking out all picturesque. What did she do, post images of it on Instagram before coming here? She has to know I don't care, right? I don't need anyone going out of their way to buy me a gift, but her kind gesture won't go unnoticed.

I wish I could properly thank her.

Except it would be better for everyone if I was wrong. She could be happy.

Painting on a fake smile, I wave. Juan may have had a point. Maybe trying to split them up was a terrible idea. Their relationship is young. Maybe he is a decent unskilled human being who genuinely cares for her. What if they are compatible? What if she's the hot mess in their relationship?

"Smells good," Aaron says with an open bun on his paper plate. I slap a beef patty on it.

"Mm-hmm! Where should I put this?" Hannah says gesturing to the gift bag.

Bold vertical stripes, thread thin straps… my drifted gaze shifts back to the present. Summer dresses are a normal occurrence for cute girls to wear at a backyard barbeque.

"I uh…" I flipping stutter. "You didn't have to uh…" I clear my throat. "Um. Thanks." Her long golden blonde hair is in a ponytail as per usual, only it is looser. Her bangs hang free. There are a few expertly precise curls around her ears that cover her rose earrings.

Simple.

Elegant.

Innocent.

Her wily gaze lifts to Aaron, nearly breaking her neck. How does she kiss the giraffe, not that I want her to, not that I should care, but if he makes her happy… I don't know. Is he worth the frequent trips to the chiropractor?

"Don't thank me yet, Benji. You haven't seen what's inside."

Oh? Never thought at my age I would be this excited to open a present.

Curious, I stare them down or up I suppose, with a perked eyebrow, then back to the gift bag. "Is it a puppy?" I rest the flipper on the tray beside the grill, digging my hand through the tissue paper.

Oh, glitter. Pleasant. This is going to be stuck to my skin for days.

Hannah bite her lip, attentively seeking out my reaction.

Crumpling the pink tissue into a ball, I unveil a cinnamon scented bottle of hand sanitizer.

"Classy." I smirk. "You steal it from work?"

I render Hannah speechless.

Aaron pats the deck rail. "Nice deck. Did your brother build it? Must be cool having—"

"I did," I mumble. I open my mouth to compliment Hannah's dress, but *useless* here has to keep up with his numbing interrogation.

"Did you build it together?"

"Nah. Well, he helped with the supports, the rest was me."

"Wait, aren't you a plumber or are you… are you both?" And Hannah's calling me the idiot. Unbelievable.

"Tools are tools. Measure, cut, screw. It's not that complicated." My eyes unintentionally drift to meet Hannah's. *Can you believe this guy?*

Hannah's snigger fades, not appreciating my observation. "So, arranged marriage huh?"

I choke, staring over her shoulder to my mother blabbing excessively to all my friends. Reading her gestures and overhearing her ever increasing excitement, it's official.

"Aarsi is such a sweetheart."

I didn't pick her. She was just older than the rest. Am I the only one disturbed by the fact the rest of these girls are under age? Sure, Mom and Dad met when they were young, but that should not translate to me marrying young when I am older.

"We've been talking for the last couple of days," my mother continues. "And oh, she will love it here in Canada."

"*Mother…*" I whisper the second word.

"Oh happy birthday, dear!" She waves back. "Are the burgers ready?"

"The tofu ones will take longer."

Aaron's phone rings. He breaks his handhold with Hannah to answer it immediately. "Yeah? I can be there. Okay, see you soon." He rubs away his grin then double taps his thigh.

Hannah turns her attention to him.

He kisses her forehead with pink in his cheeks, "My friend's moving truck just arrived. I promised I'd help unload." His gaze shifts to me, "I'd ask if you'd want to too, Benji, considering you're a strong guy, but it's your big day old man." He pats my shoulder.

Old man? Huh. I'll remember that one.

"You want me to pick you up later or...?" focusing on his girlfriend, Aaron's question trails off.

"Be quick." Hannah eyes me cautiously like I'm inflammable near loose sparks. "The party just started."

Aaron nods.

No!

They're serious, speaking telepathically with chewed lips and hopeful eyes. I cover my mouth, holding back my tongue. Her gaze follows him, walking out to his car... longingly.

Don't be stupid.
Don't be stupid.
Don't be...

Hannah blows Aaron a kiss.

He shrugs in a rush to return to his vehicle. That's it? The goddess of beauty sends her love, and he shrugs?

I'd catch it. What the heck? What could be so exciting, he parts from his girlfriend with that much ease? I can't. I just can't…

"I can't wait to meet her. Aarsi really is all that and then some." I wink to my buddy as if I knew her too well. "Maybe we should set up a call tonight. Get the ball rolling, I mean, I'm thirty now. Time is a ticking."

Chapter Ten

Hannah

I stare at the treats on display at Ice Beanie's Café, I could amore this culinary perfection all day. They're the only place in town that serves bubble tea, but they also make the biggest desserts. Date squares the size of my palm. Fixated on the plexiglass display, I shift between the gooey Nanaimo bars and the colourful cupcakes.

I should go for the cupcake, but maybe I should buy a latte and square, sit by the window and watch the cars go by.

Which one speaks to me more: the picturesque icing swirls with the rainbow sprinkles or chocolate heaven?

If I stroke my chin any more, bone will show.

The doorbell chimes behind me. Whoever is entering, struggles to shut the door. The welcome mat flips and flops until the metal latches.

"Look what the cat brought in? Benji, where have you been—whoa, looking good," the barista says, eyeing him.

I pout.

"You've lost weight," she says, stating the obvious.

I agree. It has been two weeks since his birthday barbeque, and it is as if every time we cross paths, he has more muscle tone. Not only has he slimmed down, but he is starting to have a shape. Yes, eyes on the treats... in the display case.

Speaking of treats… nope. Do not look at him!

Benji scratches the back of his neck.

"Yeah, sorry I haven't been supporting business."

"We sell soups and multigrain breads too, you know."

He bobs his head side to side. "Yeah but nothing beats those cheesecake brownies." He taps on the glass, shifting his attention to me. "Oh. Hi." He rubs his hands together apprehensively.

I wave.

"Do you make vegan treats?" he asks the barista.

She holds up her finger, motioning she'll be a moment, then walks into the kitchen.

Elbowing his side, I remind him. "Didn't you eat a burger last week? I'm fairly certain those aren't vegan."

"It's not for me."

"Oh." I pinch my fingers together. He doesn't actually have a boyfriend does he? I don't understand how a man who flirts as comfortably with me, hasn't on other girls.

Yes, to me it's a game, but I'm certain a man as social as him could have a whole roster of ladies he teases. "Who?"

"Aarsi. She's flying in tomorrow wanting to meet me, my family, see Canada for the first time." he sighs, "Not that this small town is much of the Canadian experience. Maybe I'll take her on a hiking trail or something."

Hiking this time of year would be beautiful. I haven't had anyone to show me the trails around here, but I would love to see what everyone has been blabbing about. I'm about to ask him which one, but his lips are pressed together, visibly conflicted.

"You don't sound enthusiastic about meeting your..." new girlfriend, fiancée, mail-order bride, future wife? "What am I supposed to call her?"

"I don't know... I'm stressed. I really shouldn't be here. I have a terrible sweet-tooth." He grabs his gut, though not much fills his hands. "Hence how I got in this whole mess. But uh... almost fifty pounds. Not bad, I suppose."

"Fifty pounds? I can't even lose five pounds! Good for you!"

"You don't have five pounds to lose."

Oh, now that's just modest. I'm a tad soft in places. Unlike him, I don't go out for runs, though I should. Yes, I'm a hypocrite but my feet ache after a twelve hour shift. I'll admit it is inspiring watching him jog past my apartment. I've had to duck a few times when he's checked my window. It's rather impressive considering how far away it is from his house.

His hand wrings through his thick black pompadour. For a split second I notice all the piercings and spacers around his ears. The V-neckline of his black t-shirt shows off the curls on his chest. It must be an older shirt, it seems baggy, stretched and worn, like it could tear easily...

"Sorry, what were we talking about?" he says, ogling the same treats.

"Aeri?"

"Aarsi."

I snort, oh it really is Aarsi, huh. His hands drop to his side then wrap around his torso to claw at his elbow pits.

"She sounds sweet, I guess." He furrows, like I misinterpreted him, but I know he is all bark no bite. Crude at times, but he has always kept his hands to himself. I smile, giving him the confidence to continue. "I'm not usually... dating is good too. It's not a cultural thing, it's just Mom is well... my mom and maybe this will shut her up about me not being married. Maybe it's a cultural thing. I don't know, my parents weren't arranged. Maybe this is good for me. I... I... How's Aaron? He's not..."

At the party, Aaron was only out for an hour. He returned in time to nab a slice of cake. I snicker, recalling the event. Benji's barbeque was fun. Mr. Gakhar pretended to not understand English around my boyfriend. Only because he was in a wheelchair, Aaron assumed the man was slow in the head too. Juan won the bet, whatever it was, but Aaron was mortified with embarrassment when Mrs. Gakhar snapped at him for his arrogance. Like father, like son, I suppose.

"He's fine. Just out of town for my birthday."

"Your birthday?" His swallow is audible. "Happy Birthday!" He takes out his wallet. "My treat," he offers.

"No. No. You don't have to." I shrug off his charity, but he insists, questioning me with those thick eyebrows, what I'd like. "Well that's the problem, I don't know what to pick. Should I go for the cupcake because it's my birthday and that's a birthday thing to do, or do I go for the..."

The barista returns from the kitchen, with noticeably shinier lips. Before she answers his previous question, Benji blurts, "The birthday shake, extra whipped cream and sprinkles for the lady, and an iced mocha for me."

"Thanks."

Winking at the barista, he adds, "Go to town with this one, it's her birthday."

The barista's eyebrows rise. "Happy Birthday," she says, sliding our drinks over the stone counter. "And, unfortunately, no vegan treats at this time. Though I'll look into it, just for you."

Her smile is too inviting for my tastes, causing a wave of irritation to briefly surge through me as her gaze lingers a second too long on Benji. His hair, piercings, shirt, and his dark eyes. My cheeks burn up.

Scooting closer to Benji, I whisper, "You really don't have to. At twenty-seven, birthdays aren't that big anymore. He hands the drink over.

"They can be. Cheers!" he says with a wide grin that boosts my spirits immediately.

We clink cups.

I follow him outside, expecting him to head to the parking lot, but he turns in the opposite direction. "Where's your car?" I ask, though technically it's a truck. *Pull yourself together, girl.*

"I walked here."

I palm my forehead. His house is three blocks away. "Me too. The weather is..." Perfect with the bright blue skies, puffy cumulus clouds, and the hot sunshine on our backs. "So *the girl*... what's she like? Have you met? Or talked... or..."

He sips his iced mocha. "Two emails. My mom's done most of the talking. According to her, she's perfect—that or she doesn't care who I marry at this point, as long as I do and give her what she wants."

I sip into my drink. It's a glorified vanilla milkshake infested with sprinkles, more sugary than I was expecting.

"Grandkids."

I think I choke on a cake chunk.

"I can see why you're nervous. But uh... how does this arranged marriage thing work?"

We stride along the hot pavement with synchronized steps. "I don't know. If I like her, I guess I have to propose before she leaves, but she's only going to be here for a little over a week so that doesn't give a man much time to decide."

"And you're okay with this?"

He shrugs, momentarily lost in thought. What is there to contemplate? This is crazy!

"I owe it to my parents. You wouldn't understand."

"Is it a Pakistani thing?"

"No. And I'm not Pakistani, I'm... well I'm Canadian, but my background is Indian. It's way different."

"So you don't eat curry and..."

"Wait, did you just assume because I'm... who doesn't eat curry? Really? Curry is delicious. Mango curry... Aw, just kill me now."

With a smile, I bump my elbow into his ribs, "I'll keep that in mind next time you try to sabotage me. So, pleasing the parents, arranged marriage, tell me more. What do you owe them?"

His hand combs through his hair. The short sleeves of his t-shirt ride up displaying those taut biceps. I miss my straw, jabbing myself in the cheek by mistake.

"Long story. Weather's too good, plus I wouldn't wish to spoil your day with my problems."

"My place or yours?"

"Whoa, when I said 'my treat,' I didn't mean that!"

I swat his chest. "Ew not that! Really Benji, you're such a dirty man. I meant to hang out, like we could keep walking until our legs ache or go inside where it's cool and play videogames or something."

"Or something?" he says far too optimistically.

I scowl. "Benjamin Gakhar, I will smack you so hard, they'll call me into work to fix you up."

He waggles his brows unfazed by my threat. "Kinky," he says. "You're the birthday girl. You make the demands."

I growl.

His laugh softens my frustration. "Too far?"

"Yes!" I turn my back on him, lifting my snout in the air. "Need I remind you, I am in a relationship."

His eyes lower to the ground, watching his sandals as we pace onward.

"Do you think she'll like me with all my faults?"

"What faults?"

He smirks at me like I'm full of *doo-doo*.

"All I had to do was buy you a milkshake, and now I'm on your good side? Man, I wish I figured you out earlier. Missed opportunity, huh?"

My lips part. He wanted to ask me out, for real? Like he had a genuine interest in developing a relationship with me, not just to pass the time? I think about our previous interactions, and in particular, when I turned him down for dinner for my lame date with Aaron instead.

He didn't report me. He jumped my car. He invited me over to his backyard barbeque. This milkshake! Why have we been fighting? We? Or is it only me? He's made me squirm and blush more than I thought was humanly possible. Most of all, he's even made me feel something.

"Would we have worked out though?" I ask defensively. He made himself available and in exchange I was snippy. A wave of guilt courses through me.

"Maybe. Opposites attract."

"You're not repulsed by me?"

"No? Is Aaron?"

I snicker, "No. Not really. Sometimes he acts like extra nervous. I can't tell if he's shy or if I'm doing something wrong. He's attractive, smart, friendly, and most of all patient, but..."

Benji strides are seemingly closer. On occasion, our arms brush. I over-apologize, he grins.

"He's quite friendly. We have fun, I guess." However, I don't feel comfortable opening up about everything to Aaron like I do Benji. "This girl will appreciate how easy you are to talk to... even complain. Sorry."

He chuckles. "I don't mind our back and forth banter. I like how you're willing to put up a fight. Too bad I'm always right."

"And I know everything?" I tease back, offering him a sip of my drink. "This is too sweet for me."

We trade. His forehead crinkles at his first slurp.

"Just a bit. It's funny how tastes change after going on a diet. This used to be a go-to for me."

"We can switch back if you'd like?"

He shakes his head. "You're sweet enough as is," and winks, to ensure I caught on he was speaking about me. I flutter my lashes. This eccentric man will have no trouble wooing his girl with his crummy lines.

At my apartment, we play Mario Kart for hours racing through all four tournaments. The joysticks on my Nintendo64 controllers wobble from their years of use. I give him the controller with the broken one, because I don't trust him. He seems like the type of guy to be rough.

It's a blast from the past, playing like the last two decades didn't exist, like our responsibilities don't exist. We're big kids simply having fun. I couldn't ask for a better birthday.

For supper, we rush down the street for pitas which he insistently pays for, then we hustle back to play *Super Smash Bros* and *GoldenEye 007*.

He cusses every word out there. I laugh until my stomach is ready to empty itself. His temper is... cute. It's nothing dangerous, rather an extension of his playful demeanour. Anytime he wins a round of anything, he jumps from his seat to dance, dragging me to my feet especially when we were teamed up against computers.

With a seating readjustment involving some pillow fluffing, I sink back into prime gaming position.

"I thought you didn't play video games," he says, as we're finishing up the final round of *Mario Party 2*.

"I said I didn't have the time." Today I do. "There's a difference."

With the sun setting and the first stars of night in the summer sky, he decides to power the console off. We both have played this game like a million times growing up to not care about the ending.

"Thanks for the birthday party," I say, routinely wrapping the cords around the controllers, hooking the plug-in by the Z button, and tucking them into their special caddy.

He rubs his lip. "We didn't invite, I mean... it's just us so... uh..." he swallows.

It is just us, huh.

"Aaron missed out. Where is he?"

"Business conference, I think. Seminar? I'm not too sure. He's in the city but will be back Sunday night, except I'm working so I won't see him until the next day. He wouldn't care for this, more of a mobile puzzle gamer. When I asked, he said he never played growing up, and he doesn't have any interest starting now." I tuck a loose strand of hair back into my ponytail. "He promised he'd make it up to me though. Texted me a 'Happy Birthday!' this morning. I chatted with a bunch of friends from back home too, so it wasn't like I was entirely lonely, but I appreciate your company. Sometimes Aaron can be intense. I worry I'm not a fun girlfriend, when work demands so much out of me. It makes me feel like I have to choose between him and recharging, and honestly, I think i'd rather..." I end it there. TMI. I open my mouth and close it again. I said too much.

He checks the time on his phone.

"I don't usually have people over. I haven't… I'm not like you planning a party and inviting half the town. I work all the time, so I don't. I guess you do too, except I don't try for a social life. Hanging out usually tires me out but…" *Stop rambling!*

He grins, though no sound comes out of his mouth. He's silent. Content. Me too, I suppose.

"Are you still nervous about meeting the girl?"

"The girl? You mean Aarsi?"

"Yeah."

"Just say her name."

I shake my head. "Are you nervous?"

Benji takes a deep breath. Mistakenly I watch his broad chest expand as he does so.

"Yeah. Arranged marriage is a dated practice, no pun intended." I giggle regardless. "And I don't want this town to think I'm a *freaking* creep for marrying a *freaking* child." Though he doesn't say freaking, I'm more stunned by that final word, child.

"How old is she?"

"I assumed Mom would sprinkle my name to a couple of twenty-something-year-olds, you know, the second choices, the ones who weren't swooped up, or had low standards. That's what she did in the past. I thought she would simply set me up on a blind date with some poor soul she found at a wedding. Turns out, there are agencies overseas dedicated to this type of thing. Official matchmaking services—"

"Benji, how old is she?"

"Eighteen, turning nineteen in a couple months."

I make a dramatic tug at my collar.

He nods. A thirty-year-old marrying an eighteen-year-old he never met? Yikes.

"Is she okay with that?"

"I guess. Maybe it's my culture over there, I don't know. At her age, I never thought I'd be in this predicament." Shaking his head, he stands. "I should get going. It's late. You're Aaron's girl. This is my problem not yours."

Aaron's girl.

Standing at the front door, we are face to face. I suppose he should leave. He doesn't disagree, though... "Hey um... Benji? Are you doing all this, the arranged marriage, because you feel guilty?"

"Feel?" he snorts.

I hold out my arms inviting him in for a hug. He looks like he could use one. Despite all the fun this evening has entailed, whatever is in that mind of his taunts him. With a smirk, he takes a step closer, wrapping his arms around me, accepting my invitation. My hands naturally slip around his neck, inching closer, so I can nuzzle into the crook. He's a cozy warm, but perhaps I'm the one who needed this hug with my parents living miles away, down south, while I'm here in this town on my own.

Missing that feeling of home, comfort. I'm at such ease, I tighten my grip, resting my ear on his shoulder.

Missed opportunity, huh?

He shouldn't have to marry a girl he never met. I feel his pain and I wish I could take it away from him, and make him feel at ease like he has for me today.

He pulls away, jolting me out of this daze, assessing me slowly from head to toe, darting straight to my blue eyes.

Fire melting ice.

Soaking in his darkened eyes, his right iris has more flecks than his left. And for a brief moment I wonder, what would it be like if I wasn't Aaron's girl?

Benji swallows. His lips part, like he can read my mind.

What if I were his?

Suddenly my back is pressed against his corded forearms, pressed into the wall, pressed into him, pressed like his mouth against mine. My heart lifts. I feel... oh. I feel a fluttering in places I studied in textbooks, but never experienced... firsthand.

Not like this.

He starts slow like a gentle hum across my lips, though short seconds transform it into a hostile match, where he is persistent to prove himself.

Giving his all in ruthless tenderness.

My hand opens, sliding into his hair. Such thick, thick hair, I pinch it between my fingers, twirl, pull, comb, yank, and massage my other hand down the inside of his shirt. Gravity deceives me, or no... Those are his hands lifting me up the wall, hoisting me by my... oh my. He's incredibly strong.

My brain refuses to be sterile.

My body wishes to concede.

My toes curl.

He's going to make me swear, no sweat, no wait I'm already sweating. I don't know.

He's getting married.

I'm Aaron's girl.

What are we doing? I'm not this type of person. We're not available.

Our lips part, though he leans back a second before I can conclude with a peck. Conclude? Yes. I deem it so. I have the willpower to stop, right?

I open my eyes.

His are wide, dark, beautiful, yet scared. Pushing me away, he staggers, whacking his palm on the wall to brace his rigid body as he slides on his sandals. Mortified. At who? Me? Himself? What did we… what's going on?

In a blink, the door slams and he is gone.

Chapter Eleven

Benji

In the arrivals section of the local airport, I hold a paper sign with Aarsi's full name on it. I'm at the very last place I want to be. People walking by snicker, but Mother insisted, somehow convinced the ten minute one-on-one drive to my parents' house would spark chemistry or place us in a mood.

Doubtful.

Aarsi should be able to find me immediately. I'm the only brown—no, I'm the only South Asian guy in the building. Also if Mom thinks she'll swoon into my arms within the mere minutes we're alone together, she's delusional. Dad has to put an end to all those dumb dramas she watches.

Alternating hands often, I rub my sweaty palms along my charcoal dress pants.

It was one kiss, no big deal, right?

Exhale.

Big deal! Big freak-normous deal! I can't fix this. Even if she dumps him, I'm stuck with Aarsi, that is if she understands it was a huge mistake and I'm not a homewrecker.

I think I'm going to be sick.

The plane lands, giving me another twenty minutes to nearly wet myself. I showered this morning, but I'll have to again tonight as I'm drenched in a fragrant nervous stench. Disgusting.

Deep breath. It's not like this young girl is going to be my wife, oh wait she is.

Exhale.

The air spews over my lips, the ones that ghastly mauled Hannah's. What was I thinking? I wasn't drunk. I don't drink, but... but... she gave me that friendly hug and then my mind went blank. Autopilot kicked in. If that's love drunk, I'm an alcoholic.

I'm thirty years old, but last night I was a mix between a horny teenager and a primal caveman.

She has a boyfriend! Hannah gives me a bottle of sanitizer. I give her a kiss. Nope, they are not of equal value! What the heck have I done? I should never have entered that apartment. I should have left, bought her some earrings and given them to Aaron to give to her.

I have ruined her relationship with Aaron. Yes, I was initially jealous, but Aarsi's going to step through that door any second. I don't have any other choice. Hannah shouldn't ditch her lame accountant boyfriend because I screwed up. Even so, if she let me kiss her, what if we were together and she let other guys kiss her behind my back?

Who am I kidding? This is Hannah. Everything about her is prim and proper, until yesterday.

My fault, clearly.

Why am I thinking about Hannah? I have to stop. She is not the woman I'm about to see. I am not in the right headspace for this.

Why did I allow my curiosity to have the best of me? I could've moved on not discovering how soft her lips were, or how she hangs on though she's short of breath. Her persistence is adorable, not that I should know.

Inhale.

Exhale.

It was one kiss…ing session, that's all it was supposed to be. One final hurrah before marriage, before Mom welcomed me back as her son.

One I-wonder-if moment, one I will never forget.

I step closer to the entrance.

Behind a line of impatient travellers and an elderly couple wobbling along, my 'girl' scans the room dressed in a traditionally inspired ivory tunic, with orange tapered trousers and matching gold embroidery. A sheer magenta scarf covers most of her thick wavy hair stopping well past her shoulders. Her chiffon fabric is tucked around her arms like an elegant sash.

Exhale.

I should have worn the tie. At the time, I figured the navy printed shirt and dress pants would be enough. I shaved, that has to count for something. Maybe it will make me appear younger?

Approaching the luggage pickup with a gracious stride, I swallow my breath, admiring her, or trying to. Aarsi's height doesn't boost my confidence... or lack of. At eighteen, she's a puny thing, baby-faced though with the makeup a younger Benji would have been drooling.

She's my match? Juan should be here. She'd swoon for him. They are closer in age, but I'm the one who has to make up for my past sins, or current ones.

"Aarsi!" I wave her over. "Welcome to Canada," I say in Punjabi. I'm a little rusty, and to her I probably seem heavily accented. "It's me, Benjamin Gakhar. Everyone calls me Benji. How was your flight?"

She studies me, refusing to speak until we're parked at my parents' house. Is she always going to be like this? Can she not speak any English? Is my Punjabi that off? It's going to be hard to be friends if she doesn't talk.

I squat at the planter beside the garden bench, plucking a tiger lily off its stem. I flick the aphid off, then tuck it beside the bobby pin in her hair.

"The orange matches your pants."

"My... pardon me?"

"Trousers! I meant trousers!" Right, to Grandma, pants were always underpants. *Smooth. Aren't we off to a great start.*

"Oh." She takes the flower out, twirling it in her fingers instead. "Mother tells me you are a man of many skills."

I scratch the back of my neck. "I wouldn't say many. I'm a journeyman, a plumber by..." *trade.*

"A plumber?"

"Not because I have to be. I am smart, very smart. I excelled in school, but in Canada these blue-collar jobs pay well and they're in demand all over the country... with little schooling needed."

"You're not educated?"

"I am... kind of? I completed an apprenticeship with four years of trade school. I have a steady income that could support a family. My job is stable. Don't worry. If this arrangement is a good match, I can assure you would never starve." I bite my tongue. *Don't make promises yet, you bumbling idiot head.*

Inhale.

Just forget Hannah's thighs cinched around my waist as she yanked on my hair.

Exhale.

There isn't an out from this arrangement that appeases my parents without insulting Aarsi's family, is there? Mom will know if I sabotage it and I fear how she would retaliate. Can't reject this arrangement either. Already tried and Mom wouldn't accept it.

It's pretty much a done deal. Aarsi just has to pick a wedding date, so I better make the most of this.

Her gaze shifts from my eyes to something else on my face. Is there lettuce between my teeth? A web in my hair?

"What do your ears mean?"

"My what?" My fingers graze over the piercings and spacers. "Oh. Nothing. I did that for fun."

"For fun?" Her face pales. I escort her inside hastily.

"Not fun, creative expression?" Mentioning my rebellious streak is not first date material. "You will like my family. My mother may place her demands on me but she is always charitable to guests." The door closes. "She will be a great mother to you."

Inside, we're assaulted by strong fragrances. Spiced candles litter the home, which adds to whatever aromatic explosion is wafting from the kitchen.

"Mom, Dad, Aarsi's here!" I call out in English then sneeze into my shirt. Hannah taught me the trick. Apparently bacteria will still spread to the elbow.

Aarsi flicks a cautious glance at me.

What? It's not weird. I do my laundry and despite my body odour situation, I shower daily.

Mom rushes out of the kitchen wearing traditional garb, clothes she only wears for family weddings and special occasions, vibrant makeup, and her large pendant jewellery to top it off.

Uh... okay then. I raise my eyebrows, peeking around the living room, noticing the mandarin collared shirt dad's been forced to wear.

The girls greet each other with a hug. Dad waves, watching cricket on TV, something he seldom does, and cusses like crazy when the opposing team scores or whatever one does in cricket. I never caught on to the sport. I'm a hypocrite, I know.

I dig into the fridge for a mango juice, holding one up for Aarsi. She nods.

"How was your flight, dear?"

Aarsi hangs her sash by the coats, then timidly attempts to speak English. "Good. Long. I bite small. Not go sick."

Mother slaps her chest switching to Punjabi. "You're hungry? You poor little thing, that is not acceptable. Benjamin, why aren't you feeding her? What was he thinking? Please, please, come into the kitchen and we will fill you up. Please allow me to serve you. No woman will starve under *my* roof."

"Our roof," Dad corrects.

Mom rolls her eyes, waving her hand in Dad's direction. "Yes, dear. Yes, dear." When the women pass by me, I hand Aarsi a can of mango juice. Cracking mine open, we clink. Her smile is appreciative. Cute, I guess. She's not ugly. It's just all of this is strange.

Like if our family was adopting a little sister... it would be okay, but inviting a wife? This is messed up.

There's a knock at the front. I finish chugging the small narrow can and crush it in my fist. Mom grumbles at me, hating it whenever I do that, but I drop it in the blue bin by the door. Dad leans around his seat to face the entrance though he's comfortably stuck in his recliner.

"I got it," I call out, twisting the handle. The sunshine hits my skin.

Crap! Not now!

A cold gust renders me speechless.

In baby blue scrubs that make her eyes pop, Hannah gives me a short wave, having a naturally rosy blush to her cheeks as her toes click together. Her blonde hair is tied into a tight bun with an athletically inspired gripped headband to prevent any strays from slipping out. So her. So perfect.

Unattainable.

Inconvenient.

Illicit... and kind of sexy.

"Hi," she says.

I scan the living room then shut the door behind me, so our conversation remains outside.

"About last night... I'll be quick, because I have to head to work in an hour." Yeah, even if she decided to text this, I probably couldn't reply back. All of this is too wrong. "How did you find me here?"

She points to my muddy truck and gestures to the flowerbeds. I blow out the longest exhale of my life as she nibbles on her pouty lips, while we contemplate the recalcitrant question of all: What now?

"I'm sorry. I crossed the line. We should have never..." In an attempt to ignore how effortlessly gorgeous she is I stare over her shoulder. Mom's orange tiger lilies are tall, huh. Yep, watch the bees pollinate the blossoms or the little birds chirp at each other in the hedge.

Yep, the birds and the bees.

Her audible swallow cuts me off.

"I understand, except now I can't stop thinking about it, about you, and what on earth I'm supposed to do, Benji!"

Heat fills my cheeks. I resist the urge for an encore of last night's show. "Aaron makes you happy. Don't dump him because I was a terrible friend."

Chirp. Buzz. Chirp. Buzz. Hannah's honey lips.

I squeeze my eyes shut. *There. I can't see her.*

"I let you." Her hand wraps around my wrist. I open my eyes. Fan-flipping-tastic! She had to touch me with her silky fingers? Immediately, I shake my hand free.

"But I made this happen. Hannah, we should have never been alone together. You're with someone who's going to be heartbroken if he ever finds out I... I..."

"Cleaned her pipes?" my brother's shouts from the second storey. I step down the stone path for a clearer view, finding Juan above, sitting on the ledge of his bedroom window waving his hand while deviously snickering at us.

"No! And do you mind? We're having a private conversation here!" I return to Hannah resting my hands on—no—I grip both shoulders instead. "The kiss was a mistake, okay. You and Aaron will work, just like Aarsi and I will. Albeit it requires a few well-timed romantic gestures, but we'll have to roll up our sleeves and fix this mess. My mother will rip my head off if she finds out about this, and she has eyes and ears all over town." She's a terribly social woman. "You found your Mr. Perfect. One ill-timed kiss shouldn't change the fact that you found a man who can go through a day without staining a shirt. He's a unicorn, and he's good for you."

"Are you pushing me away?"

"No..." It's not like that. This is more complicated than she realizes. I don't have a choice anymore. It has to be this way.

"Do you like her, this new girl?"

"No. It's just... ugh!" I list out my top five curses. "Don't leave him, because of what I did. That's not fair to him." *Stop touching her, even if you love how her lips feel against yours. Every flick, the taste, the pressure, the constraint, the failure, the succession, the push and pull of opposition colliding, attracting... binding.* "We were caught in the moment, we still are and it's not that I don't want to kiss you again," or that I didn't like it. I loved it. If there were no Aarsi or Aaron in this equation...

I grip the door handle instead, clenching out my frustration. "It's only... it's inappropriate and I'm a real dirtbag if we do any more behind his back. So let's nip it in the butt and—"

"Nip it in the bud."

"Bud?"

"Yeah, you don't nip butts. It's a gardening thing. You nip... anyways keep going."

I shake my head, choosing this distraction over our muddled up reality. "Do you garden? I thought you hated getting your hands dirty."

"I wear gloves."

"Huh." And without gloves? Would she dare? *Stop Benji! Sheesh man, she's taken. Unavailable. Not yours! You're not available either. You have your own butt-load of problems right now. Friend. Just friends! Stop teasing her. She isn't yours to flirt with. She never was.*

"You didn't have any plants at your place."

"They're on the porch. My roommate doesn't like having them fill up the counters. Plus, it's an apartment. I'm jealous; your mother truly has the most beautiful flowerbeds in town."

I agree. "Dad keeps her company while she's out here toiling away." Leaving the reminiscing thought, I smirk back to her. "Gardening, huh?"

"What? I can't care for plants?" she pipes back defensively.

I scratch my nose with a teasing grin. "I'm insulted you said I was dumb, but plants don't have a brain. I doubt they have a nervous system at all. Electrical pulses sure, but I'm wondering how plants are better than me."

Hannah stares down at her toes to mumble, "They smell better." While distracted, I sneak a whiff of my underarm and gag, wishing I could at the least change my shirt.

"What about skunk cabbage?"

Her grimace falters into a heavy blush.

Juan cackles, "Hey! Benji, didn't you have seeds to plant?"

We ignore him.

"Well... I do have a flowerbed at home," I offer. "That could be fun."

Hannah snickers, caressing her upper lip. "The one full of dandelions and daisies?"

"It's a self-sustaining design... monochromatic. The bees like it." I release the doorknob. "What one man calls weeds another calls herbs?" In other words, it came with the house and I haven't touched it since.

Juan guffaws. "No. Please go on about this bed you are inviting her to, at your house, you say? Will there be cultivating involved?"

I growl, cussing him out to shut up. It was much easier when he was half my height and I could toss him across the lawn or hook him by his 'pants' to the wall.

Hannah laughs at me. "That is generous of you, but wouldn't—" she cuts herself off and takes a deep breath. "I'll end it. I was wrong, I like you."

I purse my lips, hoping to nip this in the bud. And what better way than the infamous friend-zone? Any other day, I'd be flying to the moon. *She likes me. The hot girl likes me.*

"We can move on," I suggest, wishing my brain and heart were in agreement, "although I really do enjoy being your *friend*, and the only way we can proceed is if we help each other... as friends."

Juan laughs from his perch. "Unless you have the hots for each other, then this is going to crash and burn."

I cuss him out, regardless.

"Ignore him," I grumble. "Give Aaron a chance, you two have ample common ground. Also, we probably shouldn't hug." Her body feels amazing against mine. Undeniably, the cosiest feeling there is. I could spoon her for hours. If I could rewind the clock and it were honourable, and if I wasn't the most egocentric human being on the planet.

Hannah holds out her hand. "Agreed."

We shake on it.

"Who are you talking to?" Mother says to Juan upstairs.

"Benji's *friend*," not at all shying from using air quotes.

Mother joins Juan at the window sill to stare down at us.

"Oh why don't you join us for dinner?"

Hannah stares at the clock on her phone. "I should really get going..."

"No. You're too skinny. Join us! My Benjamin thinks he can hog all the food. You're starving your friends, my boy." She slaps Juan's shoulder, "Stop being useless, and put up another place setting."

I shrug, gesturing how fruitless any attempts of excusing her invites are. I mean, Aarsi's here so even her own son can't say no. I hold the door open for her like the gentleman I'm not.

Your funeral.

Aarsi sits across from me. Hannah is next to her around the crowded Gakhar dining table, her blonde hair and ivory skin like a lighthouse beacon compared to the rest of us. Mom keeps heaping more and more of the oily curry dish onto our plates, but I can barely stomach whatever the heck this is. Juan and I say nothing, drinking copious amounts of water to combat the spice. We're sweating. Man, the last time we ate food like this was at an uncle's funeral. I don't even know if he was related, we just called him uncle.

Hannah lifts her spoon with her left hand. Subtly I shake my head, waving my right hand. She squints, puzzled by my gesture, until Mom's scrutinizing glare causes her to reconsider my suggestion. She places the spoon down, picking it up with her right hand, carefully observing how Mom and Aarsi are scooping the curry into their mouth.

Her face is red, panting heavily with perspiration dripping around her brow. She's only had two bites, scraping the sauce off her rice as discreetly as possible. I restrain from laughing at her but she's trying her darn best to be polite.

"What a flavourful dish," she says, finishing her second tall glass of water.

I step away from the table to refill the water pitcher. Subtly, I place a small glass of milk beside Hannah. When I return to the table, Mother nudges me to translate for Aarsi.

"It is. However, you not need about me to worry, Mrs. Gakhar. Your dinner is mild compared to my home food."

Juan cackles, waggling his eyebrows at me. "With her cooking, I bet your Aarsi will be a flamethrower."

"Juan!" Mother hisses but Dad plays along, humming the tune of Johnny Cash's *Ring of Fire*.

Aarsi stares at me with a blank expression. "Is 'flamethrower' slang for expert cooker... chef? My cooking skills are... medium."

My grin spreads. "Sure, why not." If it weren't rude, I'd join along with Dad's crooning. I know he wants to belt the chorus. I can feel it.

"Aarsi, what a lovely tunic," Mother comments, "The embroidery is divine. What brand is that?"

"I..." Aarsi motions the act of stitching, "I made it."

"Oh how lovely! Hannah, dear. Do you sew?"

She lowers her gaze. "Just hands, I'm afraid. I wasn't one for crafts. I could never sew a button to save my life."

Mother's eyes go wide, attempting to mask her insult. Seamstressing and tailoring is Haanji Gakhar's profession, not a hobby.

Interrupted by her phone's alarm, Hannah stands, preparing to leave. "Sorry I have to run. Thank you for the meal." She bobs her head to Aarsi. "Lovely to meet you. Um..." It's just a name, but Hannah's refusal to say any foul word is downright adorable. "Wish you two the best. Benji's a great..."

Don't say kisser!

"He's great."

I exhale with relief.

At the door she shouts, "Oh and welcome to Canada!"

Aarsi leans in to whisper in my ear, "Do you have many female friends?"

How can I answer that, given I currently pushed the boundary of the word friends. Am I that obvious? Has she already figured me out? It was one kiss, can we please sweep this under the rug? I scratch my nape, tugging on my shirt collar. So hot. Can't breathe.

Mom beams at the two of us like romance is blossoming between us then answers for me. I guess that makes us her new favourite soap opera.

"He has many friends," she says proudly. "My son is very social, friendly, and generous towards those who are in need of a helping hand. When he isn't working, he volunteers his time to save the day with his handyman skills and masculine strength, too often."

Masculine strength? What the...

"He may seem like a big burly hairy beast upon the first impression, but he's a warm soul, a sweetheart. And when he cares for others, oh you will love being the recipient of that. Ooh yes. He's a cuddler."

Hmm, the words a son wishes to hear from their mother, *a big burly hairy beast*. Lovely. This is why parent chaperones are the worst, not that we need one. Okay maybe Aarsi, she is quite young, but if I was going to be frisky with a girl, she is not that girl.

Going to? Ha! I did and I screwed everything for Hannah and Aaron's relationship. I screw everything up.

Mom can boast all she wants, but the truth is I'm a bad influence.

To Juan. To Hannah. I could have been so many things and instead I'm this.. and I could have been loved by someone I care about. Instead I'm here on a date, expected to kiss Aarsi.

"Perhaps you and Hannah will become great friends over the years." Mom says to her. "You just missed it, but last weekend there were well over fifty people in his backyard for his thirtieth birthday." I scrunch my nose when she mentions my age. "Though you won't have to worry about anything. All the girls there were married or are in serious relationships. Her boyfriend is... an intellectual." Ha! Mom hates Aaron and it's all thanks to Dad's prank. Classic! Dad winks at me and I remember to breathe, easing the tension in my chest.

"His backyard? Do you not live here?" Aarsi pokes her head around the table for visual clues.

"No. He has his own house. We miss him dearly, but it is a short walk away, and I would not be surprised if after the babies come, he will want to return home."

Our jaws drop.

"What? I'm only offering to help."

"Mom. I just met Aarsi! I'm not... that's—" I can't say gross, because then she will take offense that I am not attracted to her. This entire relationship makes me cringe. "Not appropriate at this stage," I decide to say instead.

Juan laughs like a hyena.

With my darkest glare, I mutter, "Remember you're next."

Chapter Twelve

Hannah

*P*itta-tta-tah-tuh.

No! No! Please no! I headbutt my steering wheel. "Not now," I groan, rubbing my forehead against the worn leather. Why does my car have to fail at the worst of times... or all the time? Why can't I ride a bike to work like Steve? With no other option and trapped in a time crunch, I return to the Gakhar's porch passing by the roses in full bloom.

"Stay there, Pops. I got it," Benji yells from the other side. I hate how my heart flutters, recognizing the baritone of his voice.

You're Aaron's girl. I exhale, staring at my toes.

"Hannah?"

"My car..."

"Let me fetch the jumper cables and—"

"I don't have time. I'm already running late," I mumble, avoiding his dark eyes with uneven flecks. "Could you, err... I'd like to ride you—with you!"

I slap my hands over my mouth, mortified. My mind isn't like that, it's tired, and his carefree smile had me tongue-tied. Both our eyes go wide, our cheeks burning with heat. He is right, being around him is a terrible idea. The dust hasn't settled.

Aarsi joins his side, a paw hooking between the buttons in his dress shirt. One of her fingers slides between the fabrics. "Hi Hannah."

Her possessive touch shouldn't bother me, but it does, especially since I know how his torso feels under my palms. They look picture perfect together, even with the age gap. She is young and beautiful. Why wouldn't he choose her? His mother approves.

Benji gulps, breaking his blush. "It will be a minute. I'll be right back." His smirk creeps up the corner of his cheek. "I'm just helping a friend." He winks back to his mom, who clasps her hands together and sighs in admiration.

I really don't know if I can do this friends thing, but I'll try for him. Aaron deserves better than my weakness. I should break up, but if Benji can't date me then I guess I have no other choice, but to give Aaron another chance, if he will forgive me.

Juan groans.

Their dad elbows him, "Why don't you drive Hannah, so Benjamin and Aarsi will have more time together. When you get back, the two of you can bring me outside and we can have a better look at her car."

Juan rolls his eyes. "Sure. Whatever." Benji punches his shoulder on his way out the door, muttering something about trucks, or at least that's what I hope he said.

I hop into Juan's pickup.

"Where to Ice Queen?" He revs his hemi engine. I envy the power it possesses, but this is what I get for taking extra time in medical school. Debt til I'm dead.

"Just the hospital. Thanks," I whisper afraid he might hear me. Juan is one scary dude with his squint, height, and cold shoulder. If anyone is the icy one in this vehicle, it's him. The drive is silent until he backs into an empty parking stall by the hospital entrance, surprising me with his sombre tone.

"He thinks you're hot."

"Benji?"

"Yeah." His intense glare softens. "My brother will never say it, but he is *really* jealous that you're with Aaron. He's a sappy romantic too. He won't be happy with Aarsi, but he is more than capable of having her fall in love with him. I don't want him to."

"Is it because you like her?" They are closer in age.

"She's cute, I guess." He drums his fingers on the steering wheel. "No. He is my best friend and he won't listen to me, always the hypocrite giving me dating advice. You like him too."

"A bit."

"A lot. You hunted him down. He isn't perfect, but he will do everything in his strength to make your life perfect, even if that means pretending he likes your lame boyfriend." He glances at the clock on his dash. "We'll restart your battery and drop off your keys at the front desk. Actually, I'll have Benji drop them off." He winks.

Huh, maybe he's not so ice cold after all.

"Your car sucks."

Never mind. I hop out of the truck, blindly waving my gratitude as I hustle indoors.

The hours at work fly by. Although three speculations rouse relentlessly in my frazzled brain

One, Benji isn't all talk. The kiss, case and point.

Two, is there a plant with a nervous system?

And three, I should never visit Benji at his parents' house ever again. Their place is quaint. A small white house surrounded with multi-tiered flowerbeds. No wonder he was stung, it's a pollination paradise and a green thumb's dream. However, joining them for dinner was huge a mistake. Everyone was dressed up. Mr. and Mrs. Gakhar were in culturally inspired garbs and their boys were rather dashing in their form-fitting dress shirts.

Mmm... Benji in collared shirts, oh my, clean collared shirts. Navy suits him. The image lingers during my shift, contorting itself, until I'm imagining if one or two of the top buttons were to pop open revealing a little fuzz, or if I pinched the fabric, so I could drag him to my lips.

Was he consciously aware of every smirk he directed towards me? At the dinner table he seemed hungry, not for whatever the dish was, but me, the carrot dangling in front of him, in my scrubs. He could care less about Aarsi but if he did?

Aarsi and her impeccable sewing skills...

I grimace at her showing me up. Yeah, they're a perfect match for each other. Anytime Benji cuts himself up she will rush to his side, doting over him with her sewing kit.

A crude man like him, he probably only wanted that kiss from me anyways. It isn't like him and I could have ever had a real relationship. We're opposites, even if his company was the best birthday gift. That fate-bending kiss was the end of me.

Friends. Who am I kidding? Is it possible after he hoisted me by my derriere and claimed my mouth? Or was I the one to pressure him to continue? Benji is not going to repeat *that* kiss with Aarsi, is he?

The way her hands were all over him. What a conniving little... Grrr!

How am I supposed to forget? No amount of spicy curry could burn out the taste of his lips or his effortless strength.

No. Juan's a hermit. Why should I listen to him? What does his younger brother understand about love?

What do I?

What am I supposed to do about my Aaron situation? I have to fess up and end it, yet what if Benji doesn't break off the engagement, or whatever it is. How am I supposed to end a relationship with the perfect guy?

Can't ghost him, that would be rude.

What if he thinks we're more serious than I ever did, and I break his heart? No. I have to do this. I'm not in love with him and I can't be, even if we have Benji's blessing.

Uh oh. Not again.

With an embarrassing bladder dance, I duck out to the washroom. I've peed more on this shift than a pregnant woman. I should know; one of my patients tonight was eight months along. Thankfully her little one is growing healthily, and I hope the best for them.

I low key envy her. A lot of the women at Benji's birthday had bumps to brag about and adorable little ragamuffins.

Sometimes I wonder if I'd quit nursing completely or if I would work part-time if I was in their position. Everyone in my family is blonde and blue eyed. As much as I love this work and find fulfillment in it, I can't ignore the maternal parts of me. I like caring for people, but I want to care for my own people too.

I'd love to switch it up and have a dark-haired child. Picturing holding him or her with a swirl on top and patches of alopecia snuggled against my chest bundled in gender specific flannels. So cute!

Baby hands on mommy and daddy's gigantic adult hands. Aw!

I pump the foam sanitizer dispenser twice upon returning to the Emergency Room.

Steve swirls in his desk chair, "Are you alright?"

Aaron has brown hair and he doesn't feed me outrageously hot food, but is he really the man I need? I flutter my eyelashes with frustration over the three repeating speculations of recent events and exhale. I don't fit into the Gakhar family. I never will, plants don't have brains, and I'm never going to move on from that kiss.

"I guess. So any new patients?" I ask.

"There's an anxious new mom with her newborn, a rash, I think." The pen he's holding seems familiar, I check my clipboard and notice mine is missing.

Savage!

"Seems quiet for a Sunday night," I say, jinxing the station.

"Shh! Don't say that word!" Steve scolds when the phone conveniently rings.

Don't steal my pens.

"See! Look what you did!" He answers it, checks out the paperwork, then greets the new patients filling up the waiting room.

I push my apartment door open, take two steps, trip over my roommate's wedge sandals, and crash onto the couch. *You're almost there.* Too tired to continue my route to bed, I clutch the throw pillow, hugging it deep into my chest, and drift off, losing any sense of the time passing. It could be five minutes or five hours. I'm out like a light.

"Morning sunshine," Aaron whispers.

No! No! This cannot be happening.

I open my eyes. My head jerks up. Crouched next to me, he places an expertly wrapped present on my coffee table adorned in multicoloured ribbons. I shove my face into the pillow. Not now.

I want to scream. This has to be a nightmare. Wake up! Wake up!

"Hannah, I'm sorry I wasn't in town for your birthday."

"It's okay..." How is he here? Did my roommate let him in? One would assume she's dead, considering she is never around.

"Really, I want to make it up to you."

Oh believe me, you really don't. There's nothing to make up. We're even. If anything, I owe you.

"No. No. You don't have to," I say, wiping a dab of drool off the edge of my lip. Ugh! He hasn't given me enough time to figure out how I'm to go about this.

"It will be fun. We'll have dinner at my place." I sit up, curling the cushion over my chest. That sounds... romantic. I could use a heavy dose to compete with recent events. Maybe he does have a shot, if I fess up, we could start over. A private home dinner together would be the perfect place for that. We could work. He has already proven how flexible he is with my busy schedule.

Joining me on the couch, he eyes my uniform.

"Can I hug you? Are you dirty?" Benji would have said that with a shrewd smirk.

"I'm disgusting, thanks for asking."

Aaron retracts the arm he was about to wrap behind me.

"No. Thank you for the warning." He plants a chaste kiss on my cheekbone. "Would you like me to fry you an omelette before I head out to the office?"

"I'm not hungry." My teeth scrape my lip, glancing over to the wall Benji had pushed me up against, kissed me senseless, and in the throes of our passion, lifted me to his body.

"Aaron?"

"Yeah?"

"I..." *I felt nothing just now. You're a gentleman, no doubt, but I cheated on you. I kissed Benji. I made a mistake.* Guilt prevents me from staring up into his eyes and telling the truth. Any brief glance and I'm reminded of Benji's copper flecks, of his vigilant attention, the lust swirling in my gut when our lips did more than touch.

The kiss was a mistake.

Yeah, it just happened to be amazing. However, Aaron could improve with time, practice, and...

His breath hitches. "I like you too!"

I squint.

"Dinner. My place. Tonight."

Decline. Break up. Eat a tub of ice-cream instead.

"Okay," I say with hesitancy, feeling the weight of this situation sink deeper into my gut. Dinner it is.

It isn't that I don't like pink, I do, it's just I was scanning through my closet for my most feminine outfit. I own other colors too. With my hair in a loose braid, I scan my reflection through Aaron's window. My blush and glittery lip gloss adds more pink to my ensemble. Did I overdo it with the glitter? Is that dated and tacky? It seemed like a fun idea at the time. The dress is a softer shade, not peach, not nude or salmon, but cotton candy. I click my clean pristine snow white heels together like Dorothy from Wizard of Oz. I bought them for weddings, although my belated birthday could count as a formal occasion.

I sigh. I don't want to be here.

Juan begged me to dump Aaron, I couldn't agree more, but I can't trust my infected heart. If only there was an immunization shot to prevent boy trouble.

Benji is convinced I should give Aaron a chance.

The kiss was a mistake.

You're Aaron's girl.

"Oh you look darling," Aaron says, greeting me inside with a gentle side hug. Soft music plays in the background. Baby blue and ivory balloons with corresponding streamers decorate his open concept living room and kitchen. "I hope blue is okay. I had to whip this up quickly and the box of decorations my sister forked over was from her baby shower, so I had to get creative." There's tempting finger foods on stacked display dishes. Beside it is a crystal punch bowl with the matching glasses hanging off the edge. The concoction even has sliced oranges and ice—all of it straight from a food magazine.

I place a hand to my chest. "This is too perfect." Do I want perfect? Guilt roots itself in my core, growing thorns around my gut. His lips press onto my hair.

"Almost," he says with a grin.

On cue, the doorbell rings. Scratch out the candlelit dinner. He opens the door and next thing I realize his living room is packed with people I rarely know or have never met.

I can't break up with him now. What happened to the dinner? This isn't a dinner, it's a party.

Another blonde girl enters with a heavy cake box filling both arms. She's wearing a bright red shade of lipstick, complimenting her edgy look. Somehow I feel like I couldn't rock a crop top with a denim jacket. It wouldn't be modest of me.

"Hey Ronnie!" She winks up at him then tips her head acknowledging me, "Birthday girl, right? Happy day! Happy Birthday! I'd shake your hand but I'm waiting for Mr. Perfect here to clear some space on the counter."

Aaron chuckles heartily, full of life. He rearranges dishes for this other blonde and greets her with a tight embrace.

Uh... what?

He pulls from their hug in horror. "Oh no! It isn't like that. This is Tiffany; we're just friends."

I snort, covering my mouth as I peek at the cake. There's that word... friends.

The doorbell rings again. "Oh I'll be right back," Aaron says enthusiastically, answering the front door *again*.

Tiffany nudges my side. "He's great, isn't he? The two of you are adorable together. Like two peas in a pod." The thin strap to my dress slips, I slide it back onto my shoulder. Closer, she adds, "Don't be jealous. I saw that look. He and I are in the past, we really are just friends now."

I exhale, relieved from her comment. Perhaps Benji is right. It is a possibility. Maybe I don't have to dump Aaron at all. We'll let the flame die out and become merely friends. My heart may flutter when Benji enters the room, however one day we'll look back at all of this and laugh, and I'll confess to Aaron when we're happily married and that little one-time mishap will give him nothing more than a wary chuckle.

Friends is possible.

Searching for his gaze, I find Aaron's back obstructing my view, as he greets his latest guests with a civil squeeze.

Still, a side hug for the girlfriend? No. No, I'm overreacting. He planned a birthday party for me. So what, he gave me a side hug. Maybe he prefers to keep his hands to himself. It's cleaner, less messy, and simpler.

I feel a flutter in my stomach.

When Aaron steps aside and I can actually greet the guests face to face, since his towering frame isn't blocking me off, I gasp. The air in my lungs leaves my chest and I'm left momentarily speechless. It's the one person who shouldn't be here… the unwelcome guest. *No!*

Benji presses his lips together, clears his throat, and peeks on Aarsi by his side. Nothing lecherous, just protective, and not like a jealous protective. It's more like he is looking out for her, helping her navigate the strange and potentially dangerous world of small towns.

This thorn with his lanky arms attached to my side prods me.

"Happy Birthday, sweetheart!" Aaron rests his huge hands on my cheeks, and plants a forceful peck on my lips. "So? Thoughts? I hope you don't mind I invited some of my friends too. I figured since you haven't been living in town long we could make this a fun meet-and-greet." He nods at Benji and Aarsi, "Including some of your closest friends."

Closest? Ha... if he only knew.

"Sorry your roommate couldn't make it, then again you probably see enough of her."

I cackle.

"Give me one more minute, okay birthday girl or belated birthday girl. I'm going to help Tiff with the candles." Again he briefly emotionlessly pecks my lips.

Benji studies us, particularly me during and after. He pats Aarsi's shoulder, saying something in Punjabi. My guess is, "Save me a seat," as he's gesturing towards the crowded space. His body turns to me. His broad shoulders take up the room, but I don't mind. It's more of a protective wall than a blockading one. He shoves his hands into his pockets while his eyes follow his date finding a spot.

"I suppose I should have brought my Mario costume, huh?"

I flick his arm. Solid. Perfect veins for IVs.

"Why are you here? Are you trying to complicate this? You said it..." I glance around the room for unwanted snoops, "...was a mistake."

"Slow down, Peach. He invited me. It was this or an evening with the fam-jam. I'm strictly on travel guide duty. Besides, my body can only handle so much of that curry. If this keeps up, you and I are going to get real friendly in the ER. Except when I drop my pants it won't be sexy." Finally returning his focus on me, he grins wilder, "It'll be flaming *fecal matter* everywhere." Of course that isn't what he says, but I interpret it as the other.

"Language!" I hiss then I cringe, gripping my stomach in recent memory of the aftermath. "And don't remind me."

Aarsi laughs with my roommate's friend. I forget her name but she is brand new to town, newer than me. She sits on the floor next to his date, attempting to learn basic

Punjabi words. With a marker, Aarsi draws on her hands and wrists. Benji's stare moves over my shoulder to the kitchen where Aaron and Tiffany are jousting with birthday candles.

"I'd watch out for her," Benji says, sliding his sandals off next to the mountain of shoes that no one is bothering to place on the wire shoe rack.

My shrug is rigid. "They're just friends."

He gives me an incredulous look.

"No really they are. Tiffany already admitted there was something in the past, but it is long gone. She's rooting for me."

He crosses his arms.

Ex-girlfriends aren't always evil.

"Hey! Why not?"

"One. They are familiar, as in she's welcome in his personal bubble." They are standing awfully close, but so are we. "Two. Romantic or not, her relationship with him is stronger than yours." They do have clever pet... no they're just nicknames. "And three. He's not a romantic... which ties into my second reason."

"Those are terrible reasons. And... you witnessed the kisses and the sweetheart endearments. He is romantic."

Benji rolls his eyes around the crowd. "Like—" he zips his lips. "Sorry language. Like H-E-double hockey sticks he is. Anyways, agree to disagree. You have yourself a gentleman, when what you really need is a handyman." His clears his throat. At this rate I wonder if it is more than nerves, if he has sawdust stuck in his lungs. Either way, his voice deepens each time to an irresistible husky timbre. "I mean, the whole quirk of dating a perfectionist is to mess with them. Tangle their hair, wrinkle their clothes, smear their shiny, oh-so-shiny, lip gloss..."

Suddenly I'm feverish. Sweating like a pig, I wait for him to end his joke and move on to serious matters, before he ruins my party and my relationship.

"Oh yeah, bonus reason, numero four. You're both blonde and hot. Except she seems more daring, like she's your long lost evil twin sister. You know the type, rides a motorcycle, or at least poses along one in one of those skimpy bikinis you're too modest to try."

"You're not supposed to call anyone hot when you're taken, and how do you know I don't own a bikini?"

"Do you?" he asks.

I blush. Maybe I do, maybe I don't. It all depends if tankinis count. I wear a t-shirt over them anyway.

"But I've already done something I'm not supposed to. If you ask me, maybe you're the evil one. What you did seemed devilish to me." He winks.

"Stop. You have..." my gaze shifts to Aarsi drawing on more girls, "...her." She seems charismatic like him. Another point against me.

"Aarsi? It's not a bad word, it's her name. Me and my bad words, maybe we are a perfect match. I sure do have her. Wait and see, she'll be wrapped around my finger in no time, but that doesn't mean it is okay for motorcycle bikini blondie to enter your territory. The two of you are going nowhere if you don't get your hands dirty. Like we've been talking for how long? Dang, it doesn't take that long to put candles on a cake."

"Why do I get the sense you're jealous?" Tapping my foot, I'm fighting the urge to either boot him out the door or drag him into another room where he can elaborate.

"Because I am, but the more I learn to love Aarsi," he cringes at the name, "the more, I'll appreciate righting my wrongs."

"You love her? Are you even attracted to her?"

Benji snorts. "Maybe a decade ago, she and I would be in the other room making friends with faces. I'm not denying that she is hot. It's that being young and hot only lasts so long, you know?" Is his preference for me, meaning he admires my personality? He likes actually this? I'll take that as a compliment. I thought I was aggravating him.

"Well, you know, I feel it is rather hypocritical to say my boyfriend isn't romantic when you're not even flirting with her." *You're flirting with me! We both know who you want to kiss.*

"Fine. If that is what helps you and Aaron fix your relationship, I will accelerate mine." He picks at his ear flicking a silver ring, "Though you might not like it."

"That's not what I—"

On cue, everyone starts to sing the birthday song. Aaron rushes to my side with an arm wrapped around my shoulders, guiding me into his kitchen. "Make a wish," he whispers into my ear with a giddy grin.

Not that I believe in wishes, but I give it a go.

I wish Aaron was romantic.

Wishes do not come true; they are make-believe like unicorns, which Aaron is not. After the cake is divvied out on blue paper plates, I return to the living room.

"Come on; give the birthday girl a seat on the couch." Benji says, winking at my boyfriend, "After all, it is a *loveseat*." Catching onto the hint, Aaron finally sits beside me. His arm drapes behind me. It's the closest I have been with my boyfriend since the guests arrived. But could he stop tapping his foot at four hundred kilometres an hour? What does he have to be anxious over? He is the one who invited everybody.

One of Benji's carpenter buddies slaps his thighs. "No, this is a love seat. Ain't that right, *Ronnie*." He eyes up Tiffany playing with her hair. She snorts, easily dismissing him with a bop to his nose.

"Oh Reagan, you're such a goofball."

Benji balancing a bite size of red velvet cake on his plastic fork holds it out to Aarsi's lips. He murmurs softly in her ear, despite the volume level in this crowded room, I'm assuming it's along the lines of, "Try some, you'll like it."

Aarsi points to Benji's massive slice, "Is it vegan?"

"Yes."

Uh, no it's not. Hello, eggs, milk, and butter!

"Yes, this birthday cake is vegan." Catching my glare, he shrugs. "What? Have you seen the selection this town has for vegan alternatives? I'm doing her a favour."

He whispers Punjabi into her ear, brushing the loose piece of hair that had slipped over her eyes behind it. He pauses to admire the jewelled pin in her hair, gently sliding it out. Complimenting it, her, and taking his sweet time repositioning it in place.

Great, I think the other girls watching are swooning too.

My hair is in a side braid, not that Aaron plays with it. He seems too busy playing host and 'hello strangers please become acquainted with my girlfriend'.

"So how long are you in Canada for?" I ask.

Aarsi leans into Benji's translation.

"I fly out Tuesday morning."

"Which leaves us little time to show her the country. It's too bad it's summer," he adds. That's a first. I feel like I'm waiting all year for this season. "We can't take her snowboarding or out to the lakes to play some ice hockey and show her a true Canadian winter."

Aaron laughs, "No, but you could still take her to the lakes regardless. Oh! Canoeing perhaps, that's Canadian. We have friends with canoes you could borrow from."

We do?

Benji ponders the idea, stroking his shaved chin. Honestly, I prefer the two-day beard; it matches the thickness of his arms and chest. "Maybe you two could tag along, double date?"

Aaron fancies the idea, kissing my cheek. This is by far the most affectionate Aaron has been, ever since we started dating, yet I can't shake off those fabricated feelings.

My eyes meet Benji's. Does he sense it too? I catch myself biting my lip. How does he do that, know exactly when to look at me? Every glance our eyes connect. We're synced. His abrasive thumb sweeps another stray strand of Aarsi's long hair.

"You know what else is romantic... and Canadian?"
Stop staring at me!
"Camping."

Aaron stabs into his cake. "Mosquitoes don't seem terribly inviting to me."

Yes! I agree. Bugs are gross. They buzz, they spit, they bite, and sting. They fly into my face. I walk into webs. Shall I go on? Nasty.

With his arm hanging off Aarsi's shoulder, Benji's finger teases up and down her arm. "Campfires, late night swims, and sharing a tent?" He waggles his eyebrows, but I sense the comment being directed towards me. She does make cute arm candy, if he's content with a surface level relationship for the rest of his life, but he said... right, I'm Aaron's girl.

My boyfriend bemusedly tilts his head, "You're going to share a tent with Aarsi? Wouldn't it disrupt your arrangement's traditions or rules? You've only known her for two days."

He rolls his eyes, "Dang it, Aaron. That last part was a dirty joke. Just to be clear... *Prudy B. Jones*, girls tent, boys tent." Benji stabs his finger into his cake slice, licking the icing off clean from his stained fingers.

My mouth gapes.

"Wait, are we actually doing this?"

"Camping is the perfect summer activity," my boyfriend says, scanning the weather app on his phone. "And why don't you look at that? Full sun, all weekend."

Chapter Thirteen

Benji

Male end to female end, repeat. All day, all week I install PEX pipes through open walls and joists. New construction can be monotonous, but it beats family night with the new girl. I hate pretending. Mom suggested that Aarsi and I go to the movies, play board games, do normal first date stuff. I'm not sure how I'm going to handle taking her camping. Last night, we biked to the elementary school and shot some hoops. We finished the evening by the swing set, chilling, practicing our languages. She's picking up on English faster than I am learning Punjabi. Maybe we could be a language couple, always learning new words. I suppose having a travel companion wouldn't be too awful. I don't feel comfortable performing any romantic act with this woman, especially if my heart isn't in it.

On occasion I switch to French and she'll switch to Urdu. Then again, I thought English was a common language in Pakistan and India. Where did Mom find her, under a rock? She's a sweet girl, but with the weight on my shoulders, all of this seems rushed. Only yesterday, handholding became a thing; assuming it's to please Mother more than it is a reflection of our hearts. We're on friendly terms, but Aarsi doesn't like me already, does she?

Justin crimps pipes for another pristine brand spanking new electric hot water tank.

"Hey!" I holler from the adjacent room in the basement. "I said forty-eight inches, not forty-six inches."

"Do you want me to cut you a new piece?"

"Nah, just find me the pipe extender." I smirk, figuring this would be a good time to relieve the tension and stress from this never-ending week. I hear him drop his tools, they clang on the concrete floor covered with sawdust.

"One sec." He meanders outside to my work van, returning within five minutes. "Which one is the pipe extender?"

"You know it's the thingy next to the thingy."

He snaps his fingers. "Okay, I think I know what you're talking about."

No, he doesn't. Justin comes back another couple minutes later around the same time my brother Juan enters with his cut lumber.

"I can't find it? What does a pipe extender look like?"

Juan gives me an incredulous look. His co-worker Zack, carrying the other end of the load blurts, "Big knockers." They lower the boards.

Justin growls. "That's not funny!"

"Or a big booty," he adds, pronouncing it, 'boo-tay' with a bouncy twerk movement against Juan I can't unsee. "Whatever does the job."

Justin shakes his head. "Is there such a thing as a pipe extender?"

I'd wipe the tear coming from my eye, but my fingers are sticky.

"You guys are a bunch of jerks."

Zack curls a devious grin, "I suppose a jerk could do."

Juan snaps his fingers impatiently at him.

"Pen," he says, expressionless with zero intent of participating in our conversation.

Justin corrects his mistake and hands me the freshly sawed pipe piece. I pull out the measuring tape to an exact forty eight inches, then place it vertical with the two-by-four. He digs through the cardboard box for more strapping.

Placing the first piece around the middle, he says waveringly, "Hold the pipe and tell me when it's a good time to screw."

"It's always a good time," Zack blurts, tossing his pen at Juan's face. The marker slaps his cheek and falls onto the concrete. My brother scowls aggressively in response. Someone is going to die today and it's not me.

At four, Justin and I pack up for the day.

"Yo Juan, have you seen my step ladder?" I call out about ready to ditch the property.

He lifts his head. "The yellow one?"

I nod.

"Ask Zack. He probably took it." I search the jobsite with no luck in finding it. I wouldn't be surprised if Zack had already returned to the Jackson & Reiss Contracting Company's office. I drop Justin off at our shop first then head to JRCC before I can officially call it the weekend. A party boy like him is bound to bounce the second the clock chimes 4:30 PM.

Pushing open the glass doors, I'm met with a fresh blast of air conditioning. I greet the receptionist, finding Aarsi chatting with her.

What is she doing here? I purposely delayed any tactic Mother had of bringing her to my workplace. It's bad enough I've been hearing comments during coffee breaks.

Her age.

Tradition this and that.

Creative uses for her name in the crudest contexts possible.

However, she is cute in her getup. A crop top and jeans, but like the receptionist, she's missing the backpack. Wrong type of cute. Her and Simone are so freakishly young.

"Benji," Aarsi says in Punjabi, clapping her hands together. "I talked to Landon, but he said you were working with Juan, but he's not here."

She talked to Landon? The guys at the shop met her, my eighteen-year-old blind match with the baby face and the innocent doe eyes?

I lash out with a curse.

Simone taps a near empty pickle jar, wholesale size.

"Just for you, Benji. Pay up."

"What the..." I cuss again, staring at the glass jar with the pink sticky note taped to it, like it's taunting me. She flicks her waist long vibrant red hair.

"That too."

I shake my head, dropping my loose change in the newly implemented swear jar. *Imprudent freckled leprechaun, that's what you are.* Seriously, the chick is barely hitting five feet.

"Whatever." She'll have to pay for college somehow. "Is Zack still here? He's got my ladder." To Simone I warn, "He's a real pervert you know, I bet HR wouldn't care if you punched him in the face for his shenanigans."

Zack exits a side room, smacking Hank Reiss, the co-owner and the brains behind the company's shoulder.

"Thanks, Pop."

Nepotism, splendid. I mutter a cuss the grocery clerk taught me. Those Québécois really despise the church, huh.

Simone taps the jar. I drop a loonie. Smart girl, someone paid attention in French class.

"Sup Benji." His gaze immediately shifts to Aarsi. "Well hello, is she your sister?"

I snort.

"Cousin?"

I scratch my nose.

"No dude, that's Aarsi his mail-order bride." Reagan interjects, shaking Aarsi's hand. Both Zack and Reagan gravitate towards her. Simone rolls her eyes.

Aarsi politely grins back, tucking her long black hair behind her ears. They chat for a few minutes. I glare on occasion to keep them in line, more like a chaperone than a boyfriend.

"So... you're in grade twelve now?" I say to Simone.

She shakes her head. "Nope. I'm all done. So I'll be sticking around. In September, I'll start my first set of online courses." She adds grinning proudly. I suppose she is far more mature than these blokes beside us. "It's already the weekend, huh? Aarsi said something about camping. That sounds really fun."

Reading the clock above her head, I tap my date's shoulder to wrap things up, then with a scowl to Zack, I remind him about my ladder which he agrees to place in the back of my van. Aarsi slides her phone out from her purse to take more pictures. Right, because this is like a vacation to her.

The five of us smile.

I'm dreading the thought of her final day here. Apparently Mom has a friend of a friend who is a photographer. She booked a time slot for family photos when she's been hinting hardcore of something more intimate, possibly an engagement photo shoot. We're supposed to dress up in formal wear and I presume Aarsi and I will be forced to make googly eyes at each other. I bet Mom will find one of grandpa's old suits with all the sparkles and crap (just figurative this time) for the shoot too.

Approaching my parents' front door, both Aarsi and I overhear belligerent yelling, the equivalent of plates smashing or weapons drawn. She drops her hand on my arm.

"They have been arguing lots. Are they okay? Is their marriage in trouble?"

I snuff at the possibility, patting the hand on my arm. Filthy from work, I withdraw from any excessive touch.

"I'm sorry I can't translate what they've been upset over, there's too much and it comes out so fast."

"Don't worry about it. Just grab your things and be quick. If anything, it's about Juan, since he's like Mom's favourite."

She lets go except the concerned look on her face remains.

"Here, we'll enter the back door, quietly. If Mom knows you're here, she'll use you to join her side and she's a very persuasive woman." Wow I said persuasive in Punjabi. I'm improving.

Opening the back door for her, Dad's shouting carries from the living room.

"You're pushing him. You keep pushing him. You think you're pushing him somewhere good, but all you're doing is pushing him out."

"He walked out on his own. *He walked.* He doesn't deserve to and what does he do? He jabs his ears with pins and needles, drops out of a proper education, and curses with no respect for us or his heritage. Heritage! He could have been a doctor! Aarsi is what he needs."

"No. He needs our respect. He didn't grow up in our culture. His generation says a man moves out and provides for himself, which he is doing. Aarsi may be a sweet girl, but she is very young and they're not..."

"He needs a woman in his life! We've talked about this and you agree. He spends all day working with men and he is too chicken for intimacy, resorting to crass comments when she is exactly what he needs. He doesn't need more friends, he needs a lover. Aarsi is perfect for him. She will embrace him and encourage him for the years to come. He needs to let someone in, close, sentimentally close. She will show him how bloody awful that plumbing shop is and snap him back to reality. Benjamin will be lit with desire. He will have goals to achieve again."

A lover.

I consider the black half inch PEX ring I altered, not that I have any idea what her ring size is. It fits my pinkie so I shoved it in with the tightly packed luggage back at home. Mother insisted I have something if the moment arose.

And she is not far off from the truth. I am lonely. What use is being everyone's friend if there's not that one person I can confide in? The whole, "I'm content being a bachelor" thing? It's a lie. In these last couple months I want more than content, to be more than helpful, but I need someone… a special someone.

I have a reason to care.

"No! You can't use and manipulate Aarsi to form what you want our son to be. He has made his choices. We don't like them, but they're his consequences not ours. We have a love marriage, and I won't support a marriage where Benjamin is trapped further in this downward spiral of regret. Do you truly believe Benjamin will love her the way I love you? I don't think Aarsi can comfort him. She is really, *really* young, beautiful, but young. We would get our grandchildren in due time, but I want to see him happy as much as you do, if not more. Ease off."

"Naheen!"

"Haanji, ease off." Dad's tone softens, "And who knows, maybe something good will come out of this camping endeavour." Peering through the threshold, I watch him rest his hand on her thigh with a rosy glint in his eye. "You remember when we were young..."

She swats his chest.

Aarsi rushes down the stairs with a stuffed backpack, pillow, and my sister's sleeping bag. "I heard my name," she says to me with a hand on my chest.

Mom twists, Dad wheels around too, gaping at us. To put them at ease, I wrap my greasy arm around Aarsi and kiss her temple. "They were saying you're too good for me."

I smile, hurting inside. I don't want my parents to keep arguing about me. I already ruined Mom's life. I'll fake my happiness if I can grant hers.

"Benjamin," Dad's eyes lock on to mine and shift to the woman, correction, girl at my side, then back to me. "Drive safe."

Wow. Really? I thought you were on my side! I slam the door on our way out.

Hannah steps out of Aaron's car and assists him with unloading their backpacks and sleeping bags. The lake is still. When her boyfriend suggested the ones with the manicured parks closer to town, I laughed. Crowded is not romantic, nor were there any good fish in those waters.

I brought my rod in high hopes. One can't go to a lake without letting out a cast.

"Where's the canoe?" I ask, bringing the last of our tenting gear from my pickup.

Hannah stares at me dubiously, "Weren't you supposed to bring it?"

Aaron closes the trunk to the car. "Nope, that was my job, but they should be here any second now."

"They?" Hannah and I blurt simultaneously.

Aaron nods. "Yeah. Surprise!" he adds with shaky jazz hands. "What's more fun than camping out with friends?"

I excuse myself briefly to my truck pretending to grab something to only spit vulgarity like a bag's worth of sunflower seeds. I need to see Hannah in love with him, not me. How bloody difficult is it for him to want to be alone with her? I want to be alone with her. Me, Benjamin Gakhar… celibate bachelor. Can I even call myself that anymore?

Is this guy broken?

A silver truck parks next to mine with a fibreglass canoe up top.

"Sorry, I'm late." Tiffany says, hopping out of the driver's seat in bleached daisy dukes. "This thing is a beast!" She jumps and slaps the body of the boat. "Oh and the Keatons are in no rush to get it back anytime soon." She runs up to Aaron, giving both him and Hannah suffocating bear hugs.

"You two are adorable!" she squeals, pinching her boyfriend's cheek. "Ronnie, seriously where did you find her?"

Aaron invites his ex-girlfriend, how convincing. I don't buy this "we're only friends" ploy for one second. Tiffany is by far the one wild card played making it next to impossible to win the game. I loathe her type, throwing herself to the wind, ceasing the need to be properly wooed. We men need a challenge. This guy is hopeless. Not only do I have to teach him the art of seduction, I now have to keep Tiffany a mile away for a smidgen of progress.

Hannah ignores them to apply her sunscreen. She sits on the log near the fire pit, alone. Mr. Clueless doesn't pick up on her exit, so I join her, holding out my hand for a blob. Her gaze travels over my shoulder to the rustling of loose gravel behind me. Pivoting, I recognize a Jeep with two paddleboards strapped on top.

"Whaaaaa-sup!" Zack hollers over the engine, poking his head out the passenger seat. He yowls like a coyote.

"Did you invite them?" she whispers.

I shake my head.

"Then who..."

Reagan steps out of the driver's seat and pushes it forward so Simone can step out. Him and Zack are wearing tacky zippered cargo pants and oversized neon graphic t-shirts with the sleeves cut off. Because the acid wash vests weren't awful enough.

Aarsi skips over to give Simone, dressed like a normal human being, a hug. They point to the guys and giggle. I suppose some friendships are formed on few words. Hannah taps me with her sunscreen bottle.

"Houston, we have a problem. I guess we can throw out the whole romantic getaway idea out the window. Wasn't this supposed to be a double date?"

Sitting next to her, I slump my head onto my fist. "I thought I made that clear. I used those words, didn't I? Romantic? Double date?"

Hannah does a head count. "Well maybe it's a quadruple date? Four guys, four girls... this could still work... with a little matchmaking magic." Okay sure, let's see. Hannah has Aaron, I'm with Aarsi, Tiffany and Zack, which leaves Reagan and Simone. He's like seven feet and she's not even five. I'm doubtful, but it would be hilarious. Or maybe Reagan and Tiffany so that Zack is with Simone. Even then, there's a sizable age gap there. If Simone is close to Aarsi's age that would mean those guys are probably six years her senior, which could technically work.

I scratch at my hair still damp from my after work shower. "At least there are trees and it will be dark soon."

"What is that supposed to mean?"

"Well... maybe I'm being too optimistic here, but maybe he *is* into a challenge. What fun is sneaking away if there's no one to sneak away from?"

Hannah bites her lip, staring down to her sandals. "Is that what you planned for Aarsi?"

I shake my head. Maybe a kiss on the cheek when Hannah isn't looking, and if I can muster up the courage. "I don't want to scare the poor thing." We glance up at Aarsi taking more selfies with the crowd.

Hannah holds out her bottle of sunscreen to me. "Do my back."

I reject her offer, pointing to Aaron as my objection.

"He seems distracted." She rolls her eyes, landing them on her doppelganger. Tiffany cracks a joke that has the distant crowd bellowing. Aarsi smiles in an attempt to follow along.

"Then be a bigger distraction." I suggest. My gaze shifts to the bottle. "I believe in you. Besides, I have to set up the tents anyway." That's the plan.

Fall in love... not with her.

Forget the kiss I had with her.

Move on without her.

Chapter Fourteen

Hannah

Be a distraction. I can do that, but I groan inwardly first, realizing it will take drastic measures to attract my boyfriend's attention. I can't believe I'm actually doing this. With my swimsuit underneath, I slide my tank top off for more exposed skin to lather sunscreen on.

Jiggling the bottle side to side I coo, "Aaron?"

The rope in Benji's hand runs slack, causing him to tie the tarp to the tree all over again. He mutters something about ducks, or at least my brain filters a lovely story about them. Is that a blob of drool? He lifts the hem of his shirt to his mouth, to wipe it up, unintentionally flashing me with his soft abs in the process.

Zack also dips his sunglasses, soaking in the view. He whistles then nudges my boyfriend in the ribs.

Finally! Aaron clues in and joins me.

"Could you put sunscreen on my back?" I ask.

He grins, "I'll do you one better."

I perk a brow, curious. *Oh?* With my back to him, seconds later I feel a cool mist on my back.

Oh.

Facing Benji, we exchange disapproving glances. He nudges me to press on, but how?

"You should've called me sooner then you wouldn't have that gunk on your hands." Aaron says, offering me the aerosol can so I can spray my own torso.

I squirt a blob of my sunscreen onto my finger and paint my boyfriend's face with it.

Ridiculous! As much as I'd hate for Benji to say "I told you so," sometimes a girl does appreciate a man getting his hands dirty, or in this case slimy.

If skin to skin doesn't work, then seclusion should, right?

So I wait until after the tents are set and wait on the boat dock, sitting cross-legged and soaking in the hot sun. Aaron braces himself with his arm behind me and plants one of his signature chaste kisses on my cheek.

"So..." *What to say? What to say?*

Is he staring at my nose or my eyebrows? A minute passes. We have all weekend. There's no rush. I pick at the warped wood, unable to hide my irritation.

"You invited Tiffany."

"She's fun. I thought you two hit it off at the party."

We watch the activity in the middle of the lake. Zack and Reagan fight to remain stable on their paddle boards, but with Aarsi attacking Zack's legs and Simone with a firm grip on Reagan, one of them is about to... splash. Aarsi climbs on the board with Tiffany's help. She stands proud with her arms high.

"I was hoping this weekend could be... romantic." I dare not look into his eyes, not for what I need to say next.

Aaron slides his feet into the dark water.

"Oh." He drums his fingers on the dock. "Oh! Tiffany and I are just friends. I mean, we did date once upon a time, and it was serious, really serious but..."

"Aaron?" I lean closer. He pokes my butterfly hair clip, wordlessly reminding me it's sliding out of place. It was supposed to be above my brows yet the clip is dangling upside down beside my ear. I adjust it before it falls out and is lost forever.

"It was when we were younger, so you shouldn't worry."

"That pause made me worry just now."

"It's in the past."

I scowl at him regardless, because I know the feeling. I'm guilty of it.

"Well, we were heading off to separate universities and I cut things off, thinking when she did finish her teaching degree, the likelihood of her returning to the same town as me was slim."

"That sounds like you still love her."

His voice quavers, "As friends."

I cross my arms in disbelief.

"Perhaps I found out she moved back to town recently and I've been meaning to catch up. She has been with a dozen guys since, easily. It isn't like..." Aaron refuses to look at me. "*And* I didn't want to risk anything by spending time one-on-one. She can be... well... um... Tiffany."

Mm-hmm, that sigh was not subtle. What a dope. He is clearly head over heels over a woman that isn't me.

"I knew this would happen. You'd see her and... I know she's open, no bubbly, no that's not it either—"

"Pretentious?"

"Hannah! No! Tiff is not pretentious."

I mock his words like a ventriloquist's hand.

"Extravagant maybe? She has a bold personality, but that's what I love about her." Love. Present tense. He loves her, which is why we can't click no matter how hard Benji and I manipulate the atmosphere. There is no chemistry. "Therefore, the party and camping with friends seemed like less awkward opportunities than three-wheeling one of our dates."

"Except she would have been fifth wheeling if Aarsi's new friends didn't show up."

He chuckles. "Don't tell me for one second you actually believe there's something going on between them. Benji is... he's... well... for a bisexual he's awfully chaste."

My snort is so vocal; I choke up a loogie somewhere between my nose and the back of my throat. Our kiss was anything but chaste.

"Right? His mom set up the whole arrangement, yeah, so maybe that is why he is with her, because as open as he is to his friends, his Pakistani culture can't accept his gayness."

I pinch my temples. "No. He is not gay."

"And he's not Pakistani either! I'm Indian!" Benji shouts. We turn to gawk at him standing along the shore, fiddling with a tackle box and a fishing rod leaned up against the fire pit log bench thing. "Sound carries over the water, dimwit."

"Sorry," Aaron says sheepishly, lifting his feet out from the lake, to curl his arms around his bony legs.

"Oh yeah, and one more thing. Generally speaking, we tend to view that subject a tad more lenient unlike our Pakistani's neighbours, since most of them practice Islam. Sikh. Muslim. We are a very different people."

"You're not gay though, right?" I tease.

"Are you flippin' serious?" His face is blistering red with rage, though again my sun-baked brain seems to filter his vibrant vocabulary. Many of his words enter one ear and shoot out the other without fully being processed. Turning to Aaron, I swat his bare back, bald, not a hair to it.

"I know for a fact he isn't."

Whispering to me, Aaron asks, "Are you positive? He seems defensive."

I want to say that he was more offended in the Emergency Room when I accused him then, but what happens at work has to stay there. I can't tell Aaron about the kiss either. Although he did open up to me about his ex.

"I just know."

Aaron shakes his head. "I don't buy it."

"Likewise with you and Tiffany, *Ronnie*."

"Fine. I still have some feelings for her."

"Just 'some?' I'm sitting next to you in a tankini and you've been staring at her this whole time."

Benji hollers, "That's no tankini, Peach."

"No." Aaron gulps, ignoring Benji's comment. "I've been watching all of them..."

Lies!

"Aaron, has anything happened between you and Tiffany since our relationship began?"

"Hannah! Never! I wouldn't dare deceive you. I'm not a two-timing, adulterous, cheating cad. The only time I've been with her without you around was at Benji's party, the person I was helping move was Tiffany. She needed a hand. I would have recruited others, but you were all having so much fun, you especially."

Yikes, that's one tough pill to swallow. It's not enough. Please, give me one fault to balance out our wrongs.

"And you would choose me over Tiffany?"

His response is slow-coming, gritting his teeth and avoiding my longing eyes, he mumbles, "It's too early to tell."

Outraged, I stand, contemplating whether I should kick him into the water, which he's far too tall to succeed in, or belt the truth, but then he adds a, "Please forgive me."

Great. So not only did I cheat on Mr. Perfect, I'm holding him back from his true love. I am officially the worst human being on the planet. I can't seem to do anything right, not anymore. He stands next to me, pulling me into a gentle embrace as if for the sake of my happiness.

I'm done.

He may have checked all the criteria I had on my Prince Charming list, but he is not for me. I'm so stupid. Why did I put myself through this, wasting my time with him? He didn't love me, he was being polite. I was his distraction. Her replacement. Agh! I'm awful.

I am so done.

The perfect man didn't want me. I wasn't good enough for him. This whole thing was a farce.

"I'm sorry. Should I drive you home?" he offers like the gentleman he is, like he didn't admit we never had a chance.

Sniffling, I bury my face from the splashing spectators. "No."

He sighs with relief, a massive grin on his face. "Oh Hannah, you don't know how good it feels to let it all out, I've been worried for weeks, but we had only just started dating, then there was your birthday... and who wants that on their birthday?"

Weeks? Great.

Our relationship had been weeks wasted. Great.

My birthday? Great.

So that party wasn't really for me, was it? Great.

"See Benji was hoping you and I would work..." And now he's going to marry a girl he doesn't like because the woman he is in love with dated *sir too nice to let me off softly* at the wrong time. Me and my stupid heart filling with rage, me and my stupider mouth blurting, "And some small part of me hoped we could too, especially after I kissed—"

Blindly I'm shoved off the dock, my arms flap helplessly in the air as I'm dunked into the lake, jolted with icy cool water. I bob back to the surface, though my legs sink into cooler water feeling a strand of lake-weed tickle my toes. "Aaaugh!" I shriek. Or maybe it was a fish, either way it was gross. And I'm back on the dock in an instant.

"Hah! Your face. Her face, yeah? Caught her totally off guard," Benji says with his arms ready to throw Aaron in next. *Please do!* His jaw slacks, watching me return to my feet. At least someone appreciates the view.

"Hey Benji, can you give us a minute?" Aaron pleads.

I shake my head, water dripping everywhere. "Don't bother."

Somehow Benji found vegan hotdogs but like the birthday cake, he pretended the hotdog buns were kosher. I suppose after eavesdropping on the breakup and saving me from an embarrassing meltdown, he upped his flirting game with Aarsi… a millimetre.

One of us should be happy, miserably so. He still pushed me into the lake.

I sit with Simone, who's ogling Reagan like he is the next teen pop sensation, which beats sitting next to Zack who speaks more on the female anatomy than a biology textbook. Really, that boy should become a gynaecologist. Then there's Tiffany who is fully aware of the effects her female anatomy brings with her suggestive comments.

And Aaron, who apparently does respond to such a thing, just not mine.

Benji hangs his strong arm around Aarsi, cooking her dinner while seemingly passing jokes in their foreign language.

I hate it. I hate all of it.

Three boys ogle Tiffany.

I poke at the charred log, channelling my negative energy to fake positive appearances. I want to go home. This was a mistake. I hate camping. I never want to see any of their faces ever again.

Benji romances his teenage bride. The foreign words divinely roll off his tongue, not like Spanish or Portuguese. Why does he have to be so ruggedly handsome? His mangled hair, his strength, his callused hands and roped arms dinged up from cuts and scrapes. I hate him. I hate both of them. How could Aaron date me when he was still in love? How could Benji force me to try and like the guy when I just don't?

I hate that he is being far more considerate with her, than he was with me on my real birthday, like that present didn't matter, like he could repeat that with anyone, and surrenders to the first girl he is told to be with. If he is going to be like that, I shouldn't even bother. He is not anchor-your-roots material.

Why isn't he crude with her?

"So have you guys kissed?" Tiffany asks, already locking her arm around Aaron. I guess he didn't delay on sharing the news, that or sound really does carry over the lake.

Aarsi flutters her long dark eyelashes up to Benji then bashfully smiles. "Not yet."

Zack hands Reagan a five dollar bill.

"Why not? She's like smoking hot," Zack blurts, scolding Benji.

"Flamethrower hot?" she asks. Benji cringes, handing off the crispy tofu dog and places his carved roasting stick down.

"You a bad kisser or something?" Reagan teases.

Benji's gaze slits towards me without any jerking motion. Subtle, secretive, sexy, and silent.

"You have had your first kiss?"

"Of course." He gulps the second half of his water bottle and licks his lips. "Back when my parents used to drag me to all our family weddings, there was this cute girl from the other side. Each wedding we hit another base."

Reagan returns the five dollar bill. "And how many weddings did you meet?"

"Three."

I swallow, shocked by his blunt admission, until I notice the twitch in his lip when he stretches the truth.

Reagan cheers, "So close," but Benji shrugs it off easily, probably because none of it happened.

"There wasn't anything between us. The weddings were really boring. The more traditional ones last for days. I was young and stupid."

Still stupid.

Reagan hands Zack another five dollar bill. "What about you?" he asks with a playful smirk towards me.

"When I was fourteen, I caught the attention of a jock. He flirted consistently, and we went on like one date, if you could call it that, behind my parents' backs. The following school day, he kissed me in the parking lot. I was expecting a peck. It was certainly not." I cringe recalling the moment his lips parted and mine didn't. "Yes, it was quite slobbery on his part. Also, I realized how belligerent he was towards schoolwork, so we went our separate ways. I was not going to risk my flawless academic record for a boy." With a grin towards Benji I add, "Ever since, I've sworn off stupid."

"Way to shatter a man's dreams," Zack says with a hand clutched to his chest.

Simone shakes her head muttering, "Wet dreams are more like it, perv."

Zack points to her asking about her first. Like Aarsi, she shakes her head meaning that both are kissing virgins. Zack gives Reagan his money back. He winks at Aarsi, to mess with Benji. Not caring or simply used to his tomfoolery, Benji scratches his nose.

Maybe I'm emitting a dark aura, but all the guys except Benji channel in on Tiffany.

Her fingers spread wide, sucking the group into her story. "...I opened my eyes and what do you know it was Rick not Mick. I kissed the wrong twin, and they're not even identical! What about you Ronnie?" She elbows his side.

He scratches his chin, reluctant to share. She prods him again.

"It was you."

"Elaborate."

He bites his lip, checking with me first. Why should I care? It isn't like we were in love with each other. I cheated on him. He was never willing to give me his heart in the first place. Why should I care that he wasted my time. Hey, I am not going to apologize. No way! Why should I tell him? It wasn't like it was on purpose.

"She dared me to, I chickened out, then she uh..."

"I pinned him onto the carpet and we were making out, hot and heavy, for a good hour or so until his parents caught us. He was grounded for like a week." Aaron blushes, but Tiffany feeds off each second of his embarrassment. "He's not half bad, eh Hans?"

I scowl. "My name is Hannah."

"Not Princess Peach?" Benji adds with a glint to his eyes. Mysteriously, that comment cools my simmering temper. "What about you, Reiss junior?"

Zack clears his throat, jumping to his feet. "Eighth grade art class, we had a substitute. Let's just say, after some one on one at the pottery wheel, the kiln wasn't the only thing heating up."

"The teacher?" I gag.

"I call bull," Benji says waving him off. "What about you, Reagan?"

The blond giant blushes. Ooh this is it.

"First notable one, yeah? Grad year, I was playing my guitar at an open mic. Afterwards, the girl sitting front row chatted with me for like I don't know, an hour? I bought her a treat to go with her coffee. I saw her a couple times. More talking. More coffee. Then the second time I brought my guitar, she um... helped me carry it to my car."

Simone snarls, "What do you mean, helped you carry—"

"We made out in the back. This was back before I had my jeep." He holds his hands up defensively towards Simone. "She insisted. Geez, Sim, cool your—"

Her glare mutes him.

"So?" Tiffany flutters her eyelashes. "What's so embarrassing about that?"

"The next week, she ended up being my foster sister... and I saw her room. She kept a picture of me in all of her textbooks. All different pictures, like the ones you aren't aware of... yeah." He checks his wallet for cash, counting the bills he has left which at the rate he's going is not enough.

"Are you guys making bets?" Aaron asks, finally clueing in.

Zack nods. "That and campfire bingo."

"Campfire bingo?" Simone snarls toward Reagan.

The blond duo nod simultaneously, if it wasn't for Reagan's foster story just now, I'd assume they were fraternal twins. Zack pulls out a crumpled paper from his safety orange fanny-pack. "I'm in the lead so far with 'person pushed in water', and 'catch and release.'"

Simone tears Reagan's paper out of his hand, reading out loud the ones he has circled. "Swimsuit malfunction, carving roasting sticks, and forest makeout."

"Did you makeout in the forest?" I blurt, pointing to Aaron. He shakes his head, turning to Benji who also denies the action. I tap Simone's knee. She rolls her eyes bitterly with disappointment.

Reagan yanks the paper, "Wait, you're not with... sorry." He hands a five over to Zack, returning both his wallet and the paper into his fanny pack.

Benji pokes it with a charred stick. It leaves a soot mark.

"What's with the get-up?"

Zack stands on a log to pose, Reagan jumps too, dropping his elbow over his friend's shoulder. "Since everyone else besides you dry losers camp with a case of beer, and we didn't want to be the only drunk idiots on this weekend endeavour, we decided to outfit ourselves for an adventure."

Reagan spreads his hand out to the sky, selling us on their scheme. "...To the past! Twenty bucks can buy you a whole ton of crap, like this sick man purse. Dude, I'm never losing my keys ever again. You should've joined us, Benji. They had a full wall of these bad boys. It's like Batman's utility belt, but for camping."

Aarsi pulls out her phone, snapping pictures of them, of us. Benji smiles for her, yet it's fake, like the one plastered on my face. Oh, I'm not upset that Mr. Perfect dumped me, no it is far *far* worse—I think I'm in love too and it pains me that I pushed him away, that he continually gave me chance after chance but now it may be too late. We could be happy and instead we're stuck in this convoluted mess. I think I fell for imperfect, which in all ways has proven inconvenient.

Chapter Fifteen

Benji

Tents are not entirely soundproof. The guys snore, the girls giggle; therefore, I can't sleep. How can I, next to the man who shattered the heart of the most sexy yet surprisingly innocent woman to ever exist? Is she though or did I ruin that as well? Unzipping the tent, I clamber out as silently as I can, groping my way through the darkness and making my visit to the designated pissing tree.

After another thirty minutes of hopeless attempts to crash, I pick out a few of my items and saunter to the fire pit, rekindling the flame. I stare into the flames, anticipating an epiphany of some sort and fiddle constantly with the metal ring.

I don't want to marry Aarsi Goel. But how do I fall in love with her? It's not like I have a deadline, like I have to do so this weekend. How do I make this not weird? We're from separate generations, countries, languages... even if she is making significant progress on her English, I can't seem to change how I feel.

All guys are nervous before they pop the question. Maybe, it's the audience that's wearing me down. Tomorrow when I canoe her around the lake, just the two of us, maybe just maybe that seclusion will bring out a spark.

What if what I think with Hannah isn't love but lust? We were physical, but I wanted more. What if all it is between us and whatever could have been was one untimely kiss? I screwed this up, before we had a chance. Now I'm wishing I had another shot.

Hannah plunks down beside me wrapped in a thin blanket. Immediately realizing I'm indecent, I zip up my hoodie to cover up my bare chest. In the men's tent, I've already been coined with the name Sasquatch. Zack and his ultra blond hair is Yeti. Aaron, baldy, while Reagan is Patches.

Her scowl is brief until her gaze like mine fixates on the dim flames. "I'd dump my water on you, but that would be a waste of perfectly good water."

Yeah, I deserve that.

I reach my hand for hers, resting it on top. With a sigh, her head slumps to my side, resting onto my shoulder.

"Rough day, huh?" Since Tiffany's arrival, this is the first moment we've had truly alone. Another burst of laughter erupts from the girls' tent behind us. I want to give her a comforting hug, but we promised we wouldn't. The way her ex-boyfriend had acted self-righteous about not cheating on her when emotionally he was, infuriates me. If you're not available, don't date. What a dirtbag move! Dating a girl, when he's in love with someone else? That's disgusting.

Huh. I guess that's me. Well, I'm already screwed up.

"You're Sikh?" she asks, with a tilted head.

"No, I'm not. I think Aarsi is; I haven't asked, afraid of what she might think when she finds out I avoid religion." I thought it was obvious, with my haircut and how I occasionally cheat on my diet with burgers. "I think Mom told the matchmaker I am. I wouldn't be surprised if she inflated other attributes too."

Spreading her fingers wider, she invites me to lock my grip. Yes. I will and I do.

"What's that in your hand?" I clench my other hand into a fist to hide the ring.

Tents unzip, but we don't bother checking.

Minutes pass and it won't matter, because time with her can't a waste. Every moment counts, even the ones where we don't say a word.

Zack's voice booms across the lake, "Why else would I wear tear-away pants?"

"Dude, at least warn me before you flash us." That voice was probably Reagan.

Hannah and I turn to each other, speechless. Four splashes follow Reagan's absurd comment.

"Oh Ronnie, c'mon! Don't be a chicken."

Zack and Reagan support Tiffany with "bawk-bawk" clucking sounds.

"Even if the lake wasn't infested with leeches... I am not stripping because that is morally wrong. Are you crazy? I'm not skinny dipping in a cold lake. Not with you, not by myself. Swimsuits exist for a reason... No, Tiffany, I am not! You guys have fun splashing around, I'll hang here. You. Can't. Make. Me. Do. Anything!"

Hannah laughs. "I hope the lake is infested and the leeches suck him dry."

A fifth splash. Whatever Tiffany did must have been mighty convincing.

The tent behind us unzips again. Hannah and I jerk away from each other and towards the sound. If Aarsi caught us, even like this, Mother would never speak to me ever again. Our relationship would be beyond repair, and I doubt Hannah could cope with the guilt of it.

Simone rubs her eyes then shoves her hands in her sweatshirt pocket. "They're not actually..."

Weren't there five splashes?

Zack, Reagan, Tiffany, Aaron... Simone is by the tent and Hannah is beside me so that means...

Simone shakes her head, returning to the girl's tent in disgust; however, if Aarsi wasn't the remaining one in the tent that means... I hold my finger to my lips to command silence then sneak through the trees for a peek at the lake activity. Hannah follows close behind.

Two shadows buzz with activity, bobbing, treading, splashing morphing to one heart shaped blob... kissing? They're in the center of the lake. Moonlight is wary.

"Already!" Hannah gripes. I slap my hand over her mouth to silence her, yet she's quick to yank it down. "Seriously, it hasn't even been twenty-four hours and Aaron's already tongue wrestling with Tiffany... naked." She shudders.

All it takes is one wild card to make a goodie two-shoes relinquish a hearty passion. I would know. She's outright beautiful and standing in the woods alone with me.

I shake my head, pointing to Aaron climbing on the dock in haste to slip his clothes back on. Reagan cheers the kissers on.

"Unless she's kissing someone..." *else?* I can't finish that train of thought.

Tiffany climbs on the dock after him. I shift my gaze away from the newly reunited couple, meaning the two can be none other than...

"No." I lean onto the tree for support. My forehead presses into the bark. "No!" I hiss, breathing heavily through gritted teeth. We were... we were making progress. She was... lying. Aarsi doesn't care. Why would a teenager want to enter my life? This isn't about love, is it? Is it my money? I'm not *that* rich. I mean, Zack's not the guy girls would call Prince Charming, but he comes from money.

We were having fun. We were learning words. She held my hand. I didn't instigate that. I was preparing to move on and offer her my heart. Mother would have been so happy for us. She doesn't care.

"What do you mean by no? This is good. You're officially off babysitting duty."

"Babysitting... wait, what?" Shaking my head, I snap a thick branch, forcefully moving it out of my way. "No! Don't you understand?"

"That we're both single..." Her cool hand rests on my shoulder, turning me around she tugs me closer to her body by the drawstrings of my sweatshirt. "Well almost. You still have to cut it off. I suggest letting her off easy with a 'didn't feel any sparks' spiel a couple days after she flies home. Keep it tidy."

I roll my eyes and grumble. "Yeah, 'cause you'd like things to be neat and tidy." She eyes the zipper of my jacket, but I tip her chin to face me. "Except you don't understand the mess that I'm in."

What part of my life has been neat and tidy?

"Enlighten me," she coos, in that same sultry tone she had earlier today when she gave off that brief little strip-tease to that prude giraffe. Hot air billows down my hoodie. She nuzzles me, her nose scraping my thick scruff.

"You and I can never be together." I hold her close to my rampant heart. "That's the short story." I kissed her because I wanted to know what I couldn't have, just once. This would be easier if I had never bothered.

Hannah stomps on my toe, forcing me to release my hold on her. "Why do you do that?" she snaps. "Why do you love me then act like it doesn't matter, like I don't have a say in all of this? Why are you even giving her the time of day? You don't love her. You're repulsed and yet you're willing to give her a second chance. She is using you."

"Is not."

"Is so. What about her parents? What does her family have to say about her dating a man almost twice her age?"

I look away since I never asked. The question seemed redundant. Aarsi's here, yeah?

"If you keep this up, you think her parents would be supportive of their daughter moving to a country across the world?"

"They were planning on moving too, when the time was right."

"Like having you as their inside connection?"

Furious, I cook up a stew with my vile words.

"She's using your parents' hospitality for free food and board, and you as a travel guide... all she has to do is pretend to be somewhat interested in you and pay for her flight, and then it becomes a hassle-free vacation."

"I paid for her tickets..." I correct, but Hannah scowls as if that statement proves her ridiculous theory. "I had to prove I had financial means to her family. They would have paid me back in a so-called dowry."

"Why on earth would you buy her plane tickets?"

"Because my mother insisted."

"Oh so you bought plane tickets for a stranger because you wouldn't contest her? Why can't you cuss her off like you do everyone else in your life and buy us airfare? I'd say eloping to Honolulu seems mighty tempting this given second." She snarls again, like a bull ready to charge. "That's what this is all about, right? Your mom wants you to be married and have kids before you die."

"Well, you can't have children after you die," I tease to lighten the tension. I lean up at the tree, double-checking the activity in the water. Only two bodies remain, busy still... not being still. Hannah flicks my forehead. Nothing will ever make this woman slap me, huh?

"I'm being serious here, Benji. Why can't you have that with... someone else?" Her frazzled expression melts the moment her fingers pinch my jacket zipper. She stares at the metal teeth instead of my face.

I wish I could.

"I have too many regrets, Hannah. Please do not push me." See. I can ask nicely.

With two palms pressing flat onto my chest, she ignores my plea. Stepping backwards, I trip on a tree root and accidentally drag her down with me. Mud smears on my boxer-briefs.

Hannah urgently brushes the few specks of dirt off her palms, cringing from the filth. Just like this, here in the moonlight, she is beautiful. Not another sight could compare to her in my arms. A fall, sure, that's a decent alibi, but I'll pretend she is mine one more time.

I trap her before she stands, holding her down in the muck with me. She fusses over insignificant details, but I pin her close, closer, until my lips are on hers and her fuss is replaced with mews of pleasure.

"I warned you not to push me," I murmur between her persuading lips, then fuse our mouths together once again. Her palm presses into my torso. *Push.*

"It isn't like you're going to marry her."

I pull back. "What if I have no say in who Mom picks next? She won't approve of us."

"Why wouldn't your mom approve?"

"You cheated on your boyfriend."

"Besides that."

"You're paid to fondle man parts."

Her mouth gapes. "Professionally, and fondle is not the right word. If I have to see them, they're in a condition least pleasurable."

Good to know.

"I handle lady parts too."

"Yeah, that's not helping your cause."

With her sleeve tugged over her fingers, Hannah wipes dirt off my face like I'm a miscreant tot. "What's the real reason, Benji? You're not a momma's boy nor do you give anyone two-cents on anything that isn't their business. What's the long story about why we can't be together?"

I close my eyes.

"I have to know."

She picks up the black PEX ring off the ground and polishes it. Before I concede, we return to the fire pit for warmth, for her sake. I hold her hand, not like I will have the chance again. If I could have what I want, nothing would've stopped me from keeping her toasty where we were, but she is shivering and the mosquitoes are vicious.

THIRTEEN YEARS AGO

"Benjamin, slow down." Dad turns the music down as we whip down a long windy dirt path.

"It's Benji."

"No, it's Benjamin. We call you what we named you. Benjamin, slow down!"

"But there's no one on these roads."

"It's fifty and you're going one-ten!"

"Calm your tits, Dad. We're almost there." And in half the time too. Why can't he make the most of this joy-ride? Driving his truck is like riding cloud nine. It shifts like a dream. The sun is shining, the AC is maxed; there's a thick dusty cloud behind us. I'm pumped. Just him and me, father and son fishing for the whole weekend, it couldn't get any better.

Reaching over to the dash, I crank up the volume. Dad and I fight over the dial. I worked my butt for this trip. I earned it fair and square. There is no way my old man is going to hold me back.

"Calm my what? Mr. Benjamin Gakhar, don't test me."

"It's Benji!"

"Eyes on the road!"

Chapter Sixteen

Hannah

PRESENT DAY

"Benji?" I tug at his sleeve. He opens his eyes, shaking his head from what must be a haunting memory. The flames waft towards us with its smoke drying out my eyes. "What happened?"

Silence.

It isn't until the log is ash gray and spitting a few embers that Benji curses under his breath. He pokes the dying fire. "After I graduated, Dad took me out fishing to celebrate. I was valedictorian, top of my class... all that meaningless crap. Only we rolled down a steep bank ending up in the hospital," he sighs. "He lost the use of his legs; all I had were a few scrapes."

"Define scrapes." This is coming from a man who sat patiently while haemorrhaging from his thumb.

"The seatbelt bruised me a bit. At least I wasn't that dumb. Right there..." he tugs down his boxer elastic to reveal a line at his waist, "and here." Benji unzips his hoodie circling what I had always assumed was a scar from work, then rustles his hair. "Somewhere along here is a nastier mark, but it's too dark to find it at this hour." He lifts my hand into the dark mop, forcing my fingers to grope around, "It's shaped like a Y."

"What makes a Y shape?"

He shrugs, "I don't know. Maybe it was a travel mug."

Curious, I play with his hair. His scowl fades, as I indulge in each frisk.

"Can you feel it?"

What I feel is my heart beating madly to him, relaxed and susceptible to my touch. I remove my hand from his soft hair.

"Were you driving? Is that why you feel guilty?"

He nods. "It's not about feeling guilty. I am guilty."

"Accidents do happen, I face the aftermath all the time. You move on. Your parents love you regardless of your mistakes. Whether you were a good driver or not that day, you have to move on." I emphasize my concern by dropping my hand on his knee.

Benji places his poking stick down. With glassy eyes he turns to me. "It's not the accident. It's what happened afterwards." Air pushes through his clenched teeth reluctantly. "Dad and I reconciled. But Mom? The accident destroyed her life. Since his handicap wasn't work related, compo was useless and on top of adjusting to his new disability, she had to return to seamstressing full-time. It ate at her, until finally one day, she snapped at her nagging *ammi jaan*, kicking her out of the house."

"Ammi jaan?"

"Mother-in-law, but in all ways a monster. Juan doesn't remember; he was really young. I used to take him to the park, so he wouldn't have to witness them tearing off each other's heads. Grandma was a devout Sikh, but Mom sought out practicality, using the rituals that worked, and pushed aside the ones that made us outcasts. Call it hypocrisy, blasphemy, or whatever... Mom and Dad were never firm believers; it was more cultural for them."

Lifting my hand from his knee, I wipe away the lone tear of his naked confession. I need to find the positive. I met Mrs. Gakhar. She is not a monster. Difficult perhaps, but maybe that is the pain of her loss. My thumb swipes away the following tear.

"Marrying her isn't going to change the past. Benji, in all of this your mom stayed by your dad's side. This girl won't, because you're marrying out of the fear of rejection. You're afraid your mother is going to push you out like the monster-in-law, but you forget you're her son... her firstborn."

Benji blinks and a third tear trickles down his cheek.

"Listen, she's scared too."

"You don't know my mother."

"I ate enough of that scorched hot curry to recognize a mother's love. She is not pushing you away, she is tugging you back."

"Which is exactly why I must follow through on her dumb plan. If having Aarsi as my wife makes my mother happy again, as a loyal, firstborn son, I should do it." He grits his teeth like he's pissed at me for confirming his awful conviction.

I fiddle with the metal ring he dropped back when we spotted Zack and Aarsi exchanging more than friendly words. "Did you make this?" I hold out the black metal band with copper engravings exposed.

"No, I made Justin do it." He glares up to his thick eyebrows. "Of course I made it."

"How?"

"I used my engraver. Tweezers. Sat like an idiot at my dining table for over an hour. Messed up on the first two."

"What's an engraver?"

"It's a tool for engraving. I use it to carve my name on my tools. Hence engraver. Super elaborate name I know, right? I came up with it myself." He shakes his head. *I did not,* he mouths in a sarcastic manner.

My fingernail scrapes over the rough copper engraving, holding it up to the light I ask, "What does this..." I don't bother pronouncing *main tuhanu pyar karda haan* "...mean?" And how did he manage to carve all of that on it?

Inhaling deeply, he slides his dirty hands over my hair, pulling me closer. Our foreheads meet and his scruff, so near, scratches my flushed cheeks. Over my lips he whispers, "I love you." His fingernails dig into my skin and with a hitched breath, he closes his eyes. "That's what it says, I love you."

I suck in my lip, feeling the gravity of his words, and the effort tagged along with it. "That's seems like a mouthful." Then it dawns on me why he has this ring. I jump away from him tripping backwards off the log, contorted with lust and rage, a toxic envy that entices me to do far worse than stomp on his toes. "You were going to propose this weekend?"

With his head ducked down, facing the fire instead, he scratches the back of his neck. "When else was I supposed to do it?"

"Benjamin! You're not supposed to propose at all! You don't love her."

"That's why I haven't. I was waiting until I did. I'm trying… was trying." He slumps forward, avoiding my menacing glare.

"But you won't, because you..." I hastily read the ring again, "You *man two-hani pee-yard keerduh ham* me!" shoving it onto my ring finger. Aarsi doesn't deserve him. An 'I love you' on an impromptu ring, that's adorable.

He snorts, correcting me he says, "Main tuhanu pyar karda haan," but did his voice have to drop so low to tell me?

At moments like this I wish I had a shirt that said 'Talk dirty to me' with the dirty crossed out for the word 'Punjabi'. Better yet, *Speak Benji to me*. This man has his own dialect. Holding out his hand, he expects me to return the ring, but I refuse. Gripping my wrist, he tugs at the ring.

"It's stuck."

"Let me try." I command, tugging and twisting. He offers again, but I brush off his charity. "This is an everyday occurrence where I work."

"Put your hand in the lake. The cold water should loosen it up." Except my hands were cold to begin with. I'll try anyway. The ring remains wedged tight with little give to slide side to side.

Benji opens the cooler, finding the margarine meant for tomorrow's boxed macaroni and cheese. He smears it along my ringed finger and to the best of his ability underneath. That fails too.

I cunningly flutter my eyelashes. *If the ring fits...*

Benji is in a sweat, painting the evening in heartfelt vulgarities under his breath. "I need that back," he says in a panic.

"Are you serious? This is fate! This is your higher power saying your mom is wrong." Maybe this is his Bathsheba moment.

"Hannah, this isn't funny."

Extending my hand out to admire the copper ring, I add, "I like it. I think I might keep it, can I?"

He groans. "I'm too tired to fix things right now. I'm going back to sleep. In the morning, we'll drive into town."

That isn't exactly a no.

He pops into his tent, exiting with his sleeping bag bunched in his arms. I follow him into his truck with my blanket folded against my chest.

"And not drive back?" I suggest, no longer a fan of this crowd. He reclines his seat as far back as it will go. I copy him.

"No. I promised Aarsi I'd canoe her around the lake." He covers his eyes with his left arm. "I'm serious about the sleep thing. I can't pull all-nighters like I used to." His other arm drapes over the fold-down rest between our seats.

I relax my hand on top of his, teasing each knuckle, twirling the hairs, and picking at each callus and healed scab.

"I'm serious about this engagement thing." Remembering the message on the ring, I murmur in my best attempt, "Main tuhanu pyar karda haan."

There's a long silence and he's been avoiding making eye-contact the whole time. With a heavy sigh, he slides the sunroof open for a starlit view. His hand returns to mine, only slighting teasing the stiff ring into consistent rotations. "It's 'main tuhanu pyar kardi haan' for you. Kardi not karda; unless I get a sex-change, which I'm not planning on any time soon." His fingers weave between mine, locking his grip. Still staring at the inky sky, he adds, "I learned Punjabi verbally. I thought mixing the two would impress her, but it just shows how stupid all of this is. I'm pretending to be someone I'm not, and Hannah, I don't want you to pretend either. My mom won't accept this." He squeezes my hand for only a second, then returns to fiddling with the ring.

"Because?"

"*Bus*"

"Bus?"

He refuses to answer and instead turns to his side, reaching over to comb his fingers through the length of my hair, treating each strand as if it were precious silk.

"*Bus,*" he whispers.

"Oh is that Punjabi for—"

"Urdu."

"Wow. English, French, Punjabi, Urdu—is there a language you don't speak?"

"The rest," he yawns. "Sometimes where one language fails another completes the picture. There's no one perfect language." Just like there's no perfect man. The asymmetrical copper flecks in his eyes, beauty in defect.

"Why cuss?" I ask.

His lip curls up.

"It's immature."

"Age holds no restriction on idiocy. I'm young at heart, my dear." He yawns again.

I tsk. "For a person who's often referring to himself as an old man, you are acting like a child. A part of becoming an adult is stepping out into the world on your own. Who do you love? Who are you told to love? What love is it if you're forced to comply? If I had your mother's blessing—"

"You won't."

"We have to try."

"That's easy for you to say, Peach. It's not your family."

"You'll just have to give me a chance. There's always gardening. We'll start small. I will find common ground."

His fingers stop rotating the ring. I move his hand up and cup it around my face.

"Melody Oak Park," he mumbles, struggling to keep his eyelids open. With the stars and the slowed gentle tone of his voice, I can't object, albeit I'm alert, adjusted to my previous set of graveyard shifts.

"What? The one with the gazebo by the river?"

"Yeah. Meet me at Melody Oak Park on Sunday at three." He flops back into his seat. In mere seconds, the man is asleep.

I wake to a tap on the window. Cringing from the sunlight, I release my grip on Benji's hand and bury my face into the seat, snuggling into my thin blanket. Shivering, I envy the sleeping bag next to me, when the glass is tapped again.

Benji lifts his seat up, rubbing his eyes to focus on Reagan drumming an obnoxious beat on the driver's side a third time. Unsurprisingly in a grouchy mood, Benji powers down the window and cusses him out.

"Aaron and Tiffany are planning on heading out early. Did you still want to take Aarsi out for a little canoe-daling? Or I suppose..." Reagan double blinks when he confirms my identity. "Hannah?" The sunshine reflects off the copper blinding him momentarily. "What the—are you serious? Not fair. Zack, Aaron and Tiff... this has to be the weirdest camping trip I've been on."

"There's always Simone," I hint not so subtly.

Reagan laughs. "Pass. She's like a sister to me. She could never see me like that." Turning back to Benji, he leans on the open window. "Your parents are going to be pissed when they find out you're engaged to the wrong woman. No offense Hannah, you're a bombshell."

Benji rubs his sleepy eyes. "We're not engaged. She may have a ring, but I didn't propose." Reagan lifts his brow, reassessing the situation. Benji clarifies, "Hannah took it, got all pissy, and jammed it on. Now it's stuck. I went in here to sleep. There's no way in..." he turns to me, "Pardon my French, m'lady. No way in the fiery afterlife I was going back into that tent to sleep between Aaron and Zack after yesterday's events."

Noticing the tension thickening, Reagan backs away from the vehicle. Perhaps it was smoke coming out of my ears or my inflamed eyes.

"I'm not marrying you because all we've done is kiss," Benji adds, far too casually.

The kiss was a mistake. They all were!

My jaw drops. "Benjamin Gakhar, I hate you!"

"Wait—" he says, but I'm on my feet slamming his truck door behind me. "Hannah!"

"Aaron!" I scream, pacing faster, I ditch my blanket a few strides in, and run around the camp, calling out his name, until I'm wheezing at the boys' tent. Unzipping it, I cry out a whopping, "Aaron!"

"Huh? Whaa..." he mumbles, rubbing his eyes. Zack salutes me mid-change. Thankfully, due to my profession, nudity rarely fazes me anymore. In fact, I feel more out of place not wearing nitrile gloves than I do at the fact I'm invading their privacy.

"Aaron," I squat next to him cocooned in his sleeping bag. "We need to talk." Yes, we need to talk about the one thing Benji would *hate* for me to talk about. Sitting up,

Aaron reaches into his backpack and slips on a t-shirt, while seated in his sleeping bag to combat the summer morning chill.

"Hannah, you're a nice girl, but I'm in love with—"

"Tiffany. I know, I know, okay. You're perfect for each other. Great. Fan-flipping-tastic." Whoa, I almost said *that* word, the naughty one. "But I need a ride home. Now! Like can you meet up with Tiffany later, I need to tell you something, and I can't be here."

"Yeah, the guys' tent—"

My glare cuts Zack off. I'd give him an earful too, but I doubt he would care. He didn't seem to last night.

Aaron rests his hand on my shoulder, like he had for the last month, platonically.

"Tell me. I promise to listen."

"You used me, Aaron. I was looking for Mr. Perfect and you dated me with full awareness you had no heart to give. That is cold. I thought what I did was the worst, but you cheated on me before we began. What you did was wrong."

"Hannah, I never meant to... I truly was hoping to move on. Wait... what did you do?"

Nip it in the bud, girl.

"I cheated on you, Aaron. I never meant to. Really." Oh no. That could be interpreted worse than I intended. Stumbling for a rescue, I ramble on. "Honestly. It was my birthday and Benji was being a good friend... and I let him kiss me and I... I liked it."

"Uh..." Aaron drowsily scratches his head, combing his short hair with his fingers. "Me unable to get over Tiffany doesn't justify you cheating on me. You went behind my back."

"Well I'm owning up to my mistake. I am sorry. I really am. We should laugh this off. Here, I'll start. Ha. Ha. Ha. Oh Aaron you're so funny." He dodges my attempt to swat his chest. My laughter is so forced. Internally I am cringing each second that passes. "I too tried to break this off earlier, but you had to set up that birthday party, which was really kind of you, but I... I..."

"You're not better than me, Hannah. You cheated once, you'll cheat again."

"No. I thought I wanted a guy like you, that I had to prove Benji wrong. That I'm compatible with—I had a list. A Mr. Perfect list I wrote when I was in high school and you were that guy, except you weren't my guy. I'll just have to live my perfect life without you. I'm sorry. Yesterday was too peaceful. Breakups are supposed to be brash and quite frankly all of this, the cheating on each other has made me feel rather... trashy?"

"Yeah."

"Yeah? What do you mean, 'yeah?'"

"You kissed another man when we were dating. No. You're wrong. You're not perfect. Don't try to justify what you did by pointing the finger at me." He rips a strip of toilet paper, folds it, and hands it to me like it is a tissue. I use it to dab my tears. "And why Benji?"

Because I love him.

"I asked you out because you were cute and sweet, but you have by far the worst tastes. You let a guy like him, who is practically engaged to a child, kiss you while you were already in a relationship." He groans in disgust.

"Benji is a bad influence. He cusses, his whole facade, his... he is repulsive. This. You can do better. If anyone is trashy, it's him."

"Benji is not... he's... picking her over me." I wiggle the PEX ring stuck on my ring finger.

"He's making a terrible decision." A smile creeps up his cheek.

Is it a mistake though? Benji seeks redemption from his mother; I admire his desire to restore their broken relationship, but I wish there was another way. It can't be easy. They've been at this for over ten years. No, it isn't easy; it will be harder to start a family when he has drifted from his own.

"He messed up big time. He kissed you. Of course he would. It isn't like he's the caring type, you know. You're not the one who should be apologizing. Give me one minute, after this I'll drive you home, alright?"

Aaron exits the tent.

"Where are you going?"

He doesn't hear me, charging towards the water, he shouts out to Benji with an authoritative tone that causes my spine to stand up straight. Huh, so my ex-boyfriend does have testosterone.

Chapter Seventeen

Benji

Aarsi sits in the canoe waiting for me to hop in, but the blasted lifejacket just won't zip. She holds onto the dock's edge. The boat drifts into and away from the planks on the serene dark water.

"Benji!" Aaron calls out from the distance.

"Let go!" I command Aarsi.

"Did you—"

I jump into the boat, nearly flipping us out of it and into the lake. My heart races, thankful we dodged a morning polar dip. I hand Aarsi an oar, and grip mine, paddling for dear life.

"What is happening? Did you do something wrong?" she asks.

I shake my head, laughing it off. "What? No. Don't be ridiculous."

Aaron crosses his arms at the end of the dock, yelling over the waters, "I can wait here all day."

"No. It's fine. My truck has a boat rack. I can drop it off later." I holler back.

"You broke her heart!"

"No. I think you did. But I have no idea what you're talking about!" Forcing another chuckle, I wink at Aarsi. "So... did you sleep well last night?"

My date rubs her lips, "Yes."

I nod. "So... you've never been kissed?"

She scratches her cheek, focusing on her oar. *Guilty. I caught you red-handed.*

"With your upcoming flight, it would be rude of me to kiss you before you left, huh? I thought I would ask, because to be this beautiful," I try not to gag, "and yet you have never kissed a man, because you view it to be sacred, worth saving it for that someone special for the ideal moment. You would have to think about it for months, until we meet again. Could you handle the distance? Remaining chaste without me? Could you do that?"

"We could wait until our wedding ceremony to kiss."

I squint, not that she can see it. *Unbelievable.* "That would be romantic, wouldn't it? Waiting for each other. Yearning for a faithful marriage." Just for fun I add, "Since I am older, and we are on the topic of our future together. Like kissing, there's another component to our marriage we should discuss. I wouldn't dare add pressure on you, but... I've always dreamt of having a house full of kids. Five?"

"Five... um..."

"Yes. Five." I switch from Punjabi back to English. Traditionally, if a man says he wants a child, the woman must comply, I think. Dad would joke about it that way. I wait for her response, watching her squirm. This will be interesting. "At least! One after the other. Oh and twins and triplets run in my family, so we may get lucky." They don't.

"Lucky, yes..." She strokes the back of her earlobe.

"Benji!" Aaron yells from the dock.

"Even better, I could move to India so you would never have to leave your family and friends." I slow my paddling. "You'd agree I'm a fast learner. Learning Urdu can't be that difficult, not with all the progress I'm making in Punjabi spending only one week with my munchkin. Who wants to live in Canada anyways? It's so... cold."

"I like Canada." *Of course you do, you manipulative slut.*

I wait until she glances back before I blurt amorously, "I like you too."

Her eyes widen, yet her smile is delayed. Ugh, it's so forced. How could I not see it before?

"We may have to speed up this arrangement, eh?"

"Did you just say eh? I'm so proud." Okay, that comment was genuine. Her English has rapidly improved.

Returning to the dock, I continue the charade by kissing her hand before she joins the others for breakfast. Without coffee, my head is pounding. However, the con must go on.

Aaron pinches my shirt. First of all, no one threatens a Gakhar. Not me, not my brother. And heck, I may not get along well with my sister, but if anyone touched her, they'd wish they were never born. Second, after watching him kiss Hannah multiple times, horribly I may add, I'm beginning to second guess this friendship idea. No one will be asking for dating tips from the guy. Hannah is one tolerant chick. She'd have to be to fall in love with me. I really screwed this up.

Back on shore, Hannah tosses her gear in Tiffany's truck.

"You broke her heart," Aaron growls.

Yeah, I'm not scared. If I were to fight him, I'd snap him like a wishbone, but I've clearly won the girl who then ran away. The dumb giraffe is blocking my path from apologizing.

"Hearts heal. Time can never be replaced. You wasted it, man. You had a diamond and you hid her in the jewellery box." I'm back to square one with that girl. She hates me all over again. Aarsi is a con. Life is just dandy. Here I thought I was so close with this trip, but women, I may never be able to please them.

Her heart isn't the only one aching. She loathes me. If I try talking to her now, she'll blow a gasket or run further away. I have a sister; I understand there's a time to give girls space. What I wasn't expecting, is how fast Hannah can run to create that distance.

We both need our bloody coffee before we solve poverty and world hunger, okay?

Camping had to be the worst idea on the planet.

"You kissed Hannah behind my back." Aaron widens his stance.

"You want me to apologize?" I'm not sorry I kissed her. "Sorry, Mr. Pretentious," I shrug unapologetically. *Now move!*

Aaron blocks my path. He tilts his head, glaring, because just like Hannah he's too chicken to punch me. *Do it. Hit me, bro.* "You are a terrible person. Two wrongs don't make a right." Wow. That's all he's got?

"Mr. Portentous?"

"Benji... that's rude."

Like I give a clogged bowl of it. "Oh yeah, Mr. Perfect, whatever. Don't you get it? She's my Tiffany. I had to. She was miserable." He was merely caught in the middle of this. And I'm sick of him standing in my way. "More like Mr. Pain-in-my..." I grip him by his shirt collar, in a way that is truly menacing. The fabric tears as I throw him into the water. Caught off-guard, he belly flops hard. I'd be lying if the splash didn't satisfy.

I'm not sorry I kissed her. When? Sure. Why? Never.

After filling Hannah's voicemail.

After sending a long chain of texts.

After leaving a rose bouquet by her apartment door when her roommate claimed she wasn't home.

After crying like a sissy all night.

After zero sleep and zero response, I had one place left to turn for advice... my sister.

I sip my morning coffee, while I sit at my dining table in a video call with her absentminded to the fact her video is on as she applies mascara for her late night date.

"How's the love connection? Tell me, is her name really Aarsi?"

"There is no connection. She cheated on me with Zackary Reiss."

"Why would anyone cheat on you? You're a naïve sweetheart." Oh, she thinks she's funny, does she? "Who's this Zack guy?"

"You know, Hank Reiss, Juan's boss? His son, Zack—he's the type who's seen more girls than a ladies washroom." *Another tall, rich, white boy.*

"Huh. Sorry it didn't work out. Who was your matchmaker?"

"Ya… something. One sec. Let me check." I minimize the window to open my email, "Yatra Dhawan."

"Yatra! Mom hired Yatra? I told her she should hire Yasvi. If it's the Yatra I'm thinking of, she's known to match young girls willing to do literally anything to emigrate through the means of aloof wealthy Americans. Her whole business is a sham. Yes, her matches have led to marriages, but the *kids* divorce immediately. *Divorce*, Benji!"

I concentrate on my coffee, sipping it ever so slowly, yet nearly choke on her words.

"Mom said she was younger, how much younger?"

"By twelve years. She's eighteen."

My sister bursts into laughter, a screechy villainous cackle, "Eighteen. Oh wow. Aren't you like thirty now?

Mamī found you a gold digger! This is too good. Priceless!”

“Stop, okay.” If anyone is a gold digger, it’s her. She could pay my mortgage with her ex-boyfriends’ gifts. I cuss her out for it. “I can’t marry her.”

“Well Mom likes her, so you have to fix this.”

“What if I found another woman?”

“Found?” She caps her mascara to glare at me through the camera lens. “Found? Benjamin give me the goods,” she snaps her fingers impatiently. “Now! Name. Heritage. Status. Chop-chop!”

I scratch my scalp, searching for the words.

“Does she even speak Punjabi? Has she been divorced? Is she what Dad would call a charmer? How much makeup does she wear? What kind of shorts? Low-cut shirts? Does she have a tattoo? More than one? Tramp stamp? Ooh what is it? Where did you find her? Does Mom know you’ve been secretly dating exotic dancers?”

I snort, “Exotic is not the word I’d use, sorry sis.”

“Does she have a drug addiction? Do you share woes? Aw... she sounds perfect. Two losers against the world.”

Disgruntled, I end the call by slapping the laptop shut. Mom, my sister, Hannah, Aarsi... I’m having all sorts of lady trouble and I have a photo shoot I can’t be late for.

Sitting on the park bench in a pressed navy suit with a gold vest, I’m sweating buckets, anxiously tapping my foot along the path. It’s the middle of summer! I refused to wear the traditional kurta Mom suggested. I'd rather burn in Hades than have someone catch me wearing a man-dress in public. Certainly feels like I'm there in these excessive layers.

My phone clock says it's 2:57 PM.

Aarsi places her hand on my knee. "What is wrong?" Can she not feel the perspiration through the fabric?

I snort. *Like I'd tell you.* Aarsi has no clue I know about her special swim, does she? Yet she plays along with this masquerade. It's not like I have a choice. Hannah will never speak to me again because of a poor choice of words before my morning coffee. I really screwed this up. After that unwanted wake-up call from Reagan, she hasn't spoken to me since taking up Tiffany's offer to drive her into town. Cut me some slack, my heart's been torn twice mere hours apart from each event.

I wanted to leave sooner but Aarsi hadn't, so in the end, Zack won their game of bingo probably because he manipulated the playing field, and Reagan will as a result have to wear a pink bedazzled hardhat to work tomorrow. Why such a thing exists and how Zack has access to one, I'll never understand.

I check my phone clock again—still 2:57 PM.

All morning Aarsi and Mother have been doing girly things like manicures, styling their hair, and having their makeup professionally applied. If this were a blind date, what man wouldn't jump on the bandwagon? In her navy ghagra choli with gold embroidery, Aarsi is a knockout. Apparently, Mother spent long hours on these outfits while we were away.

Lipstick on a pig.

Juan assists Dad into his wheelchair from the passenger seat. Mom climbs out from the driver's side in formal attire.

Jumping to my feet, I distance myself, pacing back and forth in front of the bench.

A car pulls up beside them, not the one I was anticipating. The photographer steps out, opens the trunk to retrieve his camera bag and tripod. His assistant, which I'm assuming is a sibling or family friend, assists him by carrying the larger equipment.

Don't get your hopes up, she hates you. The magic kiss wore off, she doesn't care anymore. I ruined yet another life. I comb my sweaty hair into its distinctive swirl. I pushed one too many buttons far too many times. *Idiot! Game over!* I'm not going to be given the chance to restart the level, let alone play the love game.

My brother greets me with a fist bump and an all too knowing look.

Are you really putting up with this? Towering over me, he steps closer for his words to hit only my ears.

"What happened to that hot nurse chick?"

I shrug, peering over his shoulder to the nearby parking lot. "She hates me." Hannah refuses to respond to my calls and texts. She is completely ignoring me, not giving me a chance to redeem myself. Red roses aren't cheap, neither was the vase. I wished I could have clipped an arrangement from Mother's garden, but she'd hound me with an interrogation I'm not ready for. So I left those overpriced flowers by her apartment door when I knew she was home and waited like the idiot I am. Her car was parked by the curb. She waited longer. I had to fall for a strong-headed woman.

The photographer joins our little chatting circle, "So, what shots should we take first? Group photo or the couple shoot?"

Juan studies my anxious expression. "Let's get the family photos done first. It's bloody hot out, and I don't care much to witness my brother making kissy faces." I'd cuss him off but our mom is standing within earshot.

The photographer lines us up regardless. Mom and Dad sit on the bench, with the three of us 'kids' standing behind.

"Relax Benjamin."

"Benji," I correct.

"Sorry, Benji. Shake out your shoulders then smile."

Following his suggestions, my attention wanders away from the camera to the parking lot in dire hopes.

"Eyes back on the camera, Benji."

"My bad." I glare into the lens, like Juan, waiting for all of this to be over.

"Not so serious. Be happy." I try, but not enough by the photographer's expression. "Okay, take a step closer to your girl there." I inch closer. "Closer than *that*."

Aarsi hooks her arm around mine, gazing up at me with doe eyes. Her convincing expression takes me by surprise. My mouth gapes ajar as she snuggles into my side.

"Just like that, great. Now eyes back onto the camera... It's all very exciting but—"

A broken muffler sound distracts me, yet a few seconds later, there are still no new vehicles in the parking lot. This town's full of decrepit vehicles. Great, my imagination is desperate and playing jokes on me.

Aarsi steps out for the next few minutes for the exclusive immediate family only pictures.

Dad hums to lighten the mood, causing Mom to choke on her spit in heavy guffaw. I can't quite pinpoint which song, but it is definitely a classic.

Family. I missed this. Even if it's pretend, I play along by wrapping my arm around Juan's neck and tugging him down to my level. He tries to push me off, but I lift him, demasculinizing him tenfold as I cradle the giant like the big baby he is. Who's falling for his tough guy act now?

Mom squeals at us to stop, afraid we're going to stain our clothes. Dad pokes her in the ribs so she jumps, distracting while simultaneously wooing her to concede to our shenanigans. We'll have to edit our sister in somehow, preferably with her back to us, giving us boys the notorious stink-eye.

After who-cares-how-many-clicks the photographer points to Aarsi and me.

"Okay lovebirds, let's pack up our things and move to the gazebo down the path."

Aarsi giggles, hooking her arm around my lower back as we stride down. Like a creepy stalker, the photographer uses her sly ploy to his advantage, so I lean towards her ear and whisper, "You're not fooling anyone, Miss Goel."

At the gazebo, she grins wide, her eyes sparkling with deceit. Taking both my hands and pulling herself into my personal bubble she responds with, "Your Punjabi is off. Try again, I didn't quite catch that."

"My Punjabi? What about your English?"

"You're a great teacher." That, or my sister and I had a little chat about England's influence on her region of the country, and how English is so predominant, often street signs have it too. I figured she was from one of those isolated towns when really she has been a city girl this whole time.

"I said... I know what happened between you and Zack."

"You can't believe those rumours. Hannah is only jealous of what we have."

"Unless I saw you two with my own eyes. I hope you enjoyed your little vacation."

The photographer clears his throat to politely interrupt. "Adorable as that is... the camera is this way." We twist to face him. Aarsi pats my recently trimmed beard.

Click!

"I can't understand you. Say that again."

"I'm not your ticket to Canada. You can't use this marriage to speed up the citizenship process. The arrangement is off. When you fly home, you are going to tell your family we were not compatible and that it's over."

"What if in a few weeks, your mom finds out I'm pregnant with your child."

"She won't believe you."

"Are you certain? You and Juan hold a considerable age gap. Like father, like son."

I purse my lips. I never questioned it until I was nine and I did the math. Juan was in diapers. My parents tried to convince me that I was a honeymoon baby and born premature, but with the birth weight of nearly eight pounds and being born two months earlier than I was supposed to, that's one big fish story.

So what, I'm a love child. At least my parents were married before my sister and brother came along.

"We're not my parents." We don't have to share a heritage to be in love. I could be in love with my polar opposite.

Screw that! I am.

"But a weekend in the woods... things could've gotten a little..." Slowly, one by one her manicured fingers trail up my suit jacket. "Frisky."

"I don't give a care in the world if you try to blackmail me. I'm already the black sheep. What happens when my family finds out you are not pregnant, or worse, you are and I ensure a paternity test? You don't win."

"You're willing to break your mother's heart... again?"

I bite my lip, turning back to my Mom's beaming smile, nattering about me to the photographer's assistant.

The photographer snaps for our attention. "Benji, pretend I'm not here. You guys don't have to play shy. Kiss, cuddle, I don't care. These are your photos."

Aarsi lifts her brow, "You heard the man, kiss me." She hooks both arms over my shoulders, her fingers tease the buzzed hairs behind my neck. "You weren't the first man to kiss me and you certainly won't be the last."

I pull back before the photographer can take his shot.

Never in a million years. *I'm not your VISA.* I step away, unbuttoning my jacket, then my vest. I cuss. "It is hot out!" Removing both layers, I pop the first two buttons of my white shirt open. There's sweat stains everywhere, not flattering at all. "One sec." I drape them on the gazebo rail.

Climbing down the shale riverbank, I roll up my sleeves. Still too hot, I unbutton the third, longing for that refreshing breeze. I dip my hands into the chilled, glacier fed river, splashing my face and the back of my neck. I pinch my shirt, wafting it aggressively for the hot air to escape.

More ice cold water on my skin, and into my thick hair.

This is embarrassing; I'm being outwitted by a teenager.

"Benji?"

I turn to my right; Hannah drops the stick she was using to draw in the sandy bank only a few metres off from where I am standing. Her hair is down, blowing in all directions from the wind. Whoa, it's insanely long. Stands brush her waist, others loop around her elbows. No wonder she always has it tied back. She picks at the strays that stick to her mouth.

Her baby blues lock on me, hooking onto my heart. Thump-a-thump out of my chest like those old Warner Brothers cartoons.

Stretching out my jaw, I give her lace dress a once-over. The heavy sound of the water rushing by drowns out the rest of her words. Reeling me in, I run towards her.

"Benji, you're almost an hour late. I waited at the gazebo for like thirty minutes then—"

"Hannah!" Cupping her face, I press my lips onto hers, inhaling her last words with haste. She holds her hands out in the open. I steal one hand, navigating it around my waist. Her soft touch tickles up to my shirt's embroidered mandarin collar.

"I am so sorry!" I squeeze her into a suffocating bear hug, lifting her, swirling her into the air. "I love you! I love you! I love you! What I meant earlier, is I want the perfect proposal for you because you are the perfect woman for me. Too perfect... but don't let that stop you. We've had a few special moments, but I want you to be sure. You shouldn't marry me because you got a stupid PEX ring stuck on your finger." Oh crap, I'm rambling.

Hannah steps back. She takes my hand and plunks the damaged copper ring onto my palm. "I had to remove it for work, but I 'main tuhanu pyar *kardi* haan' you too.

I wave my hand in the air for a so-so motion. "Not quite how you say it, but we'll work on it."

"What? Aw come on! I've been practising."

"Would you like me to teach you Punjabi?"

She fiddles with the thin strap of her coin purse. "Not really. As long as you're saying something nice... or anything really." She pokes her two index fingers together bashfully. "I like the sound of it rolling off your tongue."

I take a confident stride toward her so the only space between us is reserved for our breaths and still her fiddling hands. My fingers pinch a thick untamed blonde lock of hair. "What happened to the cheerleader look? Did you run out of scrunchies?"

She blushes, playing shy. Only when she does it, my senses run wild.

"Maybe I like it when you play with my hair." Is that an invitation? Hooking an arm down her lower back, I bring her close, and our lips hastily meet once again. My question is answered when she expands the kiss. Two hands tease my mane where she so pleases. When her thumb finds the scar, she relentlessly massages it.

"Benjamin?" Mom cries out. "Where did that boy go?"

I pull back from Hannah's lips, guiding her back up to the grass, my footsteps lighter than they've ever been.

"Wait!" Hannah tugs her hand free to dig through the coin purse slung around her shoulder. "I have something." She pulls out a pink envelope that has been folded only once, evenly, sealed with a sparkly heart sticker.

She flinches when I tear it open, crumpling the thin flap that stuck to my hand, then flick it off. What? *Paper decomposes.* The wind catches the scrap, blowing it into the river's violent current. Opening yet another perfectly folded paper, I read the yellowed note... a list, noticing recent changes in red ink.

MR. PERFECT for me

1. TALL enough

2. ~~CLEAN SHAVEN~~ Fuzzy-wuzzy

3. ~~NO~~ PIERCINGS OR TATTOOS if romantic but not cliché.

4. ~~FIT~~ Strong

5. ~~RICH, LIKE WEARS A SUIT TO WORK RICH~~ Handyman

6. CLEAN VOCABULARY

7. AMAZING KISSER...

The list goes on, but I catch the drift. I'm her man.

"Fuzzy-wuzzy?" I ask. She pouts for a moment, so I peck her cheek, reassuring her. "I'm surprised this isn't in alphabetical order. Is it order of importance, if so I believe my amazing kissing skills should rank number two under my piercings.

"Alphabetical! Why didn't I..." Her mouth gapes, horrified by her flaw. "Give it to me, I'll fix it."

I crinkle it up, shoving it into my pocket. Again, she winces at how carelessly I ruined her perfect folds.

"Did you read number six?"

"Sex? Sounds fun." I wink. "I'm messing with you, Peach." One day just not today. We don't need to tarnish the Gakhar name with another love child.

"Another?"

I pop my collar.

She crosses her arms, holding back her smile with a sour expression. "I'm serious, Benji. That one isn't changing."

I cuss, watching her blush darker. She likes it.

"Benjamin?" Mom calls out in a sing-song voice.

"Did you like the flowers?" I ask.

"My roommate did, yes. In the future, buying me potted plants or taking me to the nursery, that will woo me over more so. Sorry I wasn't there, I left for the convenience store before you came by."

I kick a rock into the water. So when her roommate had said, "She's not here!" Hannah wasn't actually at her apartment. Oh. I make a mental note to slip a package of flower seeds in the first card I'll mail her.

"And what about my messages?" I ask.

"My phone died because I lost my charger. Well I didn't lose it. My roommate did, so by the time I bought a new charger... at the convenience store, checked your messages, I figured we'd talk it over in person. Because… well… I wanted to be with you… in person."

My grin stretches so wide it hurts.

"Hence the hair and the sans-makeup look."

She couldn't be more beautiful.

"You want to ditch the photo shoot and watch a movie or something?" I offer, tugging at my shirt again. This heat is unbearable.

"Or something," she repeats back, teasing the gold chain of her impractical bag. "Something like…" she points over the rock wall to the park where my family is calling out my name. "No more secrets. Let's make this official."

Official?

Taking a deep breath, Hannah gives me the reassuring nod, and I breathe easier—only slightly.

Here goes nothing.

She holds my hand for balance as we hike up the riverbank. In her sandals her footing slips, but I immediately brace her in my arms, grounded in an unwavering stance. She nods, climbing up to the grass on her own.

"Hey Mom, you remember Hannah, right?" I say, meeting the crowd waiting for me on the path leading up to the gazebo. She stands behind Dad in his wheelchair. It doesn't take Dad long to clue in. With a minor head tilt, he questions our relationship.

I nod.

But a nod isn't enough. I slip my fingers between Hannah's, holding her hand tightly not caring the heat is generating a sweat that glues them together. We reconciled, and this crazy for who knows why, this—*my* woman loves me.

Hannah smiles at me, sharing the same nervous energy. "I'm his fian—"

"Girlfriend," I blurt. Whispering in her ear, I remind her, "Let's not get ahead of ourselves." While I'm there, I kiss the sensitive flesh behind her ear, striving to give her goosebumps. "It's one thing to paralyze a man, but I'm not giving my mother a heart attack."

"It's okay. I know how to resuscitate her."

"How about you give me mouth to mouth later?" I squeeze her hand. I am quite serious about that request.

"We don't actually do mouth to mouth anymore. People puke. It's gross."

I open my mouth then close it. Repeat. Open. Close. Speechless. How does a man respond to that?

Aarsi points to Hannah and I. "Is she your girl-friend or... girl-lover?" Dang, she is an incredible actress.

"Girlfriend," I repeat, "As in..." I kiss her again, in public, and it's so freeing. No more lies or secrecy. Not to myself or my parents, especially not to the woman I love. From here on out we're vowing to be an honest couple. Neither of us pretends as we relinquish those suppressed feelings. Hannah loses her balance, but I catch her in my embrace. Our lips pull apart. "...the woman I am madly in love with."

Amazing kisser: check.

"Madly?" Hannah repeats with a twitched brow.

I shrug, it's not like I can say my favourite verb with my mother present.

Aarsi squints, crossing her arms unimpressed. Her manicured fingernail taps her skinny bicep contemplating how to respond.

The photographer scratches his head. "If you're his girlfriend, then who the heck are you?" He points to Aarsi.

Mom fumes.

My handhold isn't enough. With a scowl and my arm now protectively resting along Hannah's shoulders, I strengthen my stance. Dad wheels around to face his wife, gesturing for her to crouch to his level. He whispers a brief message in her ear, and her wrath subsides… for now.

Mom spins back to Juan leaning against a tree in the shade. She jerks her head towards Aarsi.

Juan lifts his hands up defensively.

"Whoa! Whoa there! I ain't taking Benji's sloppy seconds." He tips his head to Aarsi to mutter in Punjabi, "No offense cutie, you're just not my type."

In the midst of all the drama, Dad wheels over to the photographer and points to Hannah and I. "You're still on the clock."

Assuming this photography session is bust, Hannah hooks her pinkie with mine.

Main tuhanu pyar karda haan. With a side glimpse, I kiss her upper lip. My arms wrap around her waist, pinching her lacy dress. Buzzing in close proximity, I'm in the one place in this world that matters… with Hannah.

Click.

Epilogue

Benji

TEN MONTHS LATER

"Did someone call a plumber?" I enquire, barging into my smoking hot girlfriend's apartment. I do so covered in a day's worth of grime and without my shirt. With the door open wide, I pose, holding my adjustable wrench over my head, flexing my well-earned biceps. Not only did I lose all that excess weight, I earned myself some solid muscle mass thanks to encouragement from my sexy jogging partner. However, it means nothing if I can't show off this hard-earned progress to her.

The living room is empty.

"Where are you, Peach?" I strut down the hall in the small chance she is hiding.

"Is someone there?" the voice carries through the bathroom door. "One second."

Waiting ever so patiently, I lean up against the white walls, probably marking them up with sawdust and pipe grease, whatever is on my skin after a full day of residential repairs.

The door creaks open, revealing a long-legged woman wrapped in a towel. Her red hair is damp, draping over her right shoulder. She licks the top row of her teeth, excited.

"What the—" Repulsed, I lose balance falling off-kilter. For the full year I've known Hannah, this is the third time I've seen her roommate in person. The woman is a ghost.

Collapsed on the ground, I ask. "Where's Hannah? I just texted her."

"Called in to work."

My phone beeps. I read my incoming text. "Uh... I'll be back later then."

"I'd hope so." Her roommate winks. *Much later!*

Leaving their apartment, I sigh. "I guess it's plan B."

Returning to my truck, I swap the dirty wrench for a clean t-shirt then drive to the hospital, picking Dad up along the way. He grants me an awesome parking spot, and I wheel him towards the ER waiting room.

"Showtime," I say, patting his shoulder.

The automatic doors invite us in.

My dad starts to groan, flailing his arm in various directions. He whacks an uptight parent 'by accident.'

Little melodramatic, don't you think? I say in a head tilt, noticing beside him a familiarly tall guy.

"Aaron?" I jerk back in surprise staring at his swelling black eye. "What are you doing here? What happened to your face?"

"Adding machine."

Rolling my eyes, I pick up the receiver from the wall. Dad chokes, hisses, slurs, shouting bizarre fragments of gibberish, a few insults in Punjabi, anything to create a scene.

"Help! My dad's having an episode! He can't walk. His words are slurred. He—"

Steve, the short man-nurse dwarf-warrior guy opens the door, gesturing for us to enter. I step out of his way for him to wheel my dad into the private room.

I wink at my big man. *Way to go, Pitā, getting the special treatment.* He should forget my earlier comment; that was an Oscar winning performance.

Hannah leaps out of her office space, reaching for my shoulder. "Is everything alright? What was the trigger? What's going on?"

Still pretending to be roused by the series of events, I comb my fingers through my thick hair frantically.

"Can we talk in private?"

"Yeah, yeah. Of course. I was just writing up some paperwork, but it can wait," she says, leading me to an unused room. Guessing by the few hairs on the periwinkle sheet, her or one of the other nurses were planning on sanitizing the area. Hannah yanks at the curtain for further privacy.

"You remember what you told me when we first met?"

"What does this have to do with your dad?"

"No. That's not what you said. And my dad is fine. He's just acting."

Hannah clenches her pen so hard it cracks. "What? You mean there's no emergency?"

"No. There is... but you didn't say that either."

"Just hurry up. I have to return to work, and deal with real emergencies, with actual lives at stake."

Yeah, yeah. Pulling sticks out of people's behinds. Whatever. She drops the pen in the trash can. Extra peeved, probably because she guards those things with her life. Apparently it's a dog eat dog world when it comes to stationery in the ER.

I plant my feet, emphasizing I won't leave until she says those magic words.

"I called you a dumb plumber."

"Before that."

"I said you had herpes. Please don't remind me, okay? Hardee har har. The joke's over. It's not funny anymore."

I shake my head. "You told me to..." I wave my hand out hoping for her to finish the sentence. I suppose it has been a year, so I drop a hint, hooking my thumbs into my belt loops like a cowboy gesturing for onlookers to fix their attention towards his large belt buckle.

She shakes her head in disbelief, laughing to herself, then finishes with a sigh. "Okay Benji, drop your pants."

I grin wide. "Gladly." I unhook my belt, and drop my dirty canvas work pants. With the markers, Leatherman, and other bits, my pants rapidly hit the ground with a thud. A loose screw wheels across the laminate flooring.

"What are you wearing? Is that a..."

"Banana hammock? Yes. And it's giving me a... wedgie." I hold back my language, skipping my favourite word, because that red sign behind her head tells me to.

"I was going to say man-thong but..."

I spin around for her to read my last minute scribbled, 'Will you marry me?' on my left butt cheek. 'Slap hard for yes' fills the other cheek. Bending more to check for her reaction, my angel is beet red, pinching the bridge of her nose.

"I'm not..." She gulps. "You can't make me..." Taking a deep contemplative breath, "You brat!"

I smile wide using my grin to evade her full-blown wrath and I blow her a kiss, to irk her a teensy weensy more. "Come on babe, you know you want to hit me." I waggle my eyebrows. "Take your shot."

She steps closer with her hand way up in the air, swinging it full force.

"Aaaaugh!" she squeals. I turn around, zipping up my pants. "That really hurt. Did I hurt you?"

I shrug, snickering.

She slapped yes!

Beaming so wide, unable to curb my excitement, I cup her face for a sensuous kiss to highlight this momentous occasion, but she pulls back midway through.

"I'm covered in germs."

My thumb stokes her flushed cheek.

"Diseases..."

"So?" If anything, I'm covered in more life-threatening bacteria than her. My lips part, enjoying the splendor of my future wife for a full minute of propitious bliss. Hannah flicks my top lip, concluding with a peck on my nose.

"I have to head back to work, but after I demand it all. Roses, fancy dinner, tablecloth... clean shave, or straight-up clean... the both of us need showers. It has to be perfect and that ring better have a diamond."

"It does *and* this one fits."

"Can I see it?"

"Later. I'd hate to get 'germs' all over it."

Reaching for her hand, I hold her back from her shift for only a few seconds longer. "And I'm not a dumb plumber. I'm just a plumber. I was accepted into university, I just never went. Truth is, before the accident I had plans of entering med school, becoming a doctor. So the fact you're a nurse, it's really cool and I admire you more for it. This field wasn't meant for me, but you're exceptional at it." I don't know why I had never told her before. "I stuck with my summer job, stayed home to start my apprenticeship, because it paid well and I wanted to contribute to my parents' income loss rather than accumulate years' worth of student loans for a job I'd equally hate." I remind her for the millionth time.

She flutters her long eyelashes upset by what the clock says above my head. "That's great, but can we talk about this later?"

"Oh yeah, sorry." I release her hand. "Go save a life."

She bops my nose. "Go plunge a toilet."

Meet the Crew!

Why laugh at one, when you can laugh at them all?
Check out the rest of the *Your Blue-Collar Romance* series.

Take Your Shot
At Your Convenience
Your Attention Please

The Callous Cowboy

**He's wrangling with the laws of nature,
but she's grown on him.**

Grant Thorne prefers to hold himself accountable to a traditional set of values. He won't change for anyone, not even himself. He especially won't for a vegan. But when this cattle farmer is paired up with one for his cousin's summer wedding, he is consistently overrun with conflicting views and emotions.

However, Stella cares too much for her best friend and for the planet to read his signals. Soon she is head to head with the stubborn livestock murderer and their budding attraction with each other.

What begins as defending his family and ranching lifestyle, soon becomes a sobering wake-up call for Grant to move on and live his life, not merely preach it.

*Receive your FREE copy of **the Callous Cowboy (Romancing a Thorne)** eBook when you subscribe to Ria Zen's email newsletter.*

About the Author

Ria lives in Northern British Columbia. She enjoys the small-town charm with her handyman husband and children. She tends to geek over superheroes and cartoons. When she isn't writing or addressing immediate mothering tasks, she often returns to a life of home renovations and to her sewing machine.

Bookbub: Ria Zen
Facebook: Ria Zen
Goodreads: Ria Zen
Instagram: @riazen.author

More From Ria Zen

Holiday Escapes Series
Christmas in Pursuit (Oliver & Rachel)
Making the Getaway (Lance & Iris)

Romancing a Thorne Series
The Jolly Jester (Jesse & Collette)
The Flirty Felon (Jaxson & Melanie)
The Callous Cowboy (Grant & Stella)
The Lovelorn Lawyer (Bryson & Valerie)

Your Blue Collar Romance Series
Take Your Shot (Benji & Hannah)
At Your Convenience (Juan & Ashley)
Your Attention Please (Zack & Raven)

Standalone
Never Kiss a Demon (Jamie & Natalia)
Love and BethleMayhem (Evan & Beth)